**"*We'll* look until we find Tadeo."
Erin held out her hand to Adam,
and he took it.**

"You're too nice to me, Red. I don't deserve it
after the way I've acted."

"You're right. I *am* too nice to you, and you
don't deserve it. But we're neighbors. You're
not going anywhere, I'm not going anywhere,
so getting along makes it easier. Otherwise
we'd have to build a real fence between our
properties, and I like the view on your side."
More than she would admit to him.

He chuckled. "You
know that?"

"Is that a complime

"It just might be."

Hand in hand, they walked down the dark
path, looking for Tadeo, calling his name.
Occasionally they separated, went off in
different directions to search, but always came
back together in a matter of a minute or two.
And each time the way her hand slipped so
naturally into his…it felt right to him. Such a
simple thing, yet such a significant one.

Dear Reader

Many things come to mind when you think about Jamaica—tropical breezes, calypso music, soul-satisfying food, those exotic fruity drinks with paper umbrellas... But, for me, my first thought of Jamaica is family. Years ago I had the rare pleasure of meeting a beautiful family from Jamaica: husband, wife, seven children, all devoted to each other. Everything a family should be.

When I decided to set a book in Jamaica I knew the theme of my book had to be the strength of family. In FROM BROODING BOSS TO ADORING DAD I threw in some of those tropical breezes, some calypso music and that amazing island food, but I also brought together doctors Adam Coulson and Erin Glover, as well as a little island waif, Tadeo Reyes, and pitted them against some overwhelming and nearly devastating odds to become the family they were meant to be.

The late humorist and author Erma Bombeck said of family: 'The family. We were a strange little band of characters, trudging through life sharing diseases and toothpaste, coveting one another's desserts, hiding shampoo, borrowing money, locking each other out of our rooms, inflicting pain and kissing to heal it in the same instant, loving, laughing, defending, and trying to figure out the common thread that bound us all together.'

That common thread is love. It's where every family begins. Welcome to Jamaica!

Wishing you health and happiness

Dianne Drake

PS I love hearing from readers. Feel free to e-mail me at Dianne@DianneDrake.com

FROM BROODING BOSS TO ADORING DAD

BY
DIANNE DRAKE

Wishing you health & happiness!

Dianne

MILLS & BOON

First published in Great Britain 2011
Harlequin Mills & Boon Limited,
Eton House, 18-24 Paradise Road, Richmond, Surrey TW9 1SR

© Dianne Despain 2011

ISBN: 978 0 263 88587 3

Harlequin Mills & Boon policy is to use papers that are natural, renewable and recyclable products and made from wood grown in sustainable forests. The logging and manufacturing process conform to the legal environmental regulations of the country of origin.

Printed and bound in Spain
by Litografia Rosés, S.A., Barcelona

Now that her children have left home, **Dianne Drake** is finally finding the time to do some of the things she adores—gardening, cooking, reading, shopping for antiques. Her absolute passion in life, however, is adopting abandoned and abused animals. Right now Dianne and her husband Joel have a little menagerie of three dogs and two cats, but that's always subject to change. A former symphony orchestra member, Dianne now attends the symphony as a spectator several times a month and, when time permits, takes in an occasional football, basketball or hockey game.

Recent titles by the same author:

THE BABY WHO STOLE THE DOCTOR'S HEART
CHRISTMAS MIRACLE: A FAMILY
FOUND: A MOTHER FOR HIS SON
DR VELASCOS' UNEXPECTED BABY

CHAPTER ONE

ERIN looked at the letter she'd looked at a dozen times before, huffing out an impatient sigh as she crammed it back into her purse. This was such a waste of time, and the one thing she didn't have these days was time. She'd made the man a fair offer. Promised him every penny he'd asked, then raised that by ten percent when he'd refused... refused, *after* he'd accepted. But he'd refused the second offer too, then come right back and accepted it, yet refused her the deed when he'd been paid, and that's what was making her angry. She owned that land now. It was hers, and he was trying to pull paradise right out of her hands, at least that's what the letter stated. He was reconsidering. *Reconsidering.*

It wasn't like he'd had another offer on the property that had come in late and beaten hers, because her Realtor had been very specific about that. Hers was the only one. No one had bested her. After all, how many people needed an old missionary medical compound on a beach? Not only that, but one located in one of the non-tourist areas of Jamaica? It was hidden away, not easily accessible. Those were fairly restrictive conditions, which were exactly what she wanted.

Apparently, Adam Coulson didn't agree with her, though, because he'd dangled the perfect place like holding out a carrot for a hungry rabbit, and when she'd snapped at it, he'd pulled it back. And now, after the deal was done, he was *reconsidering*. Well, as far as she was concerned, there was nothing for him to reconsider, and she was here to get what was rightfully hers. All she wanted was her property, not a long, drawn-out court battle, since this Coulson had, essentially, swindled her by taking her money and refusing her the land deed. If he handed it over once she found him, good. She'd walk away. But if he didn't…first, she'd have to find a way to calm her nervous stomach and mushrooming case of aggravation. Then she'd engage the man in the fight of his life. It was just that simple.

"Excuse me. I'm looking for Adam Coulson," she said to the bartender. Good-looking man. Broad shoulders, casually long sandy hair. Eyes the color of the ocean, not green, not blue, but a little of both. All nice, all well worth looking at, but the scowl on his face and the fact that he turned his back on her, not after she'd spoken but *while* she was speaking, painted the real picture of him, and he certainly didn't add up to the rest of the pleasant ambiance at Trinique's.

Trinique's was a beach-side shack. Rundown, but friendly…except for the bartender. Loud, calypso-type music played in the background. Plastic crabs and fish dangled on fishing line from the ceiling, along with fishing nets and green glass floats, none of which looked like they'd ever seen a drop of ocean water. Obviously, this wasn't a place for tourists, like so much of the rest of the island was, as the drinks were served in plain glasses, not in the fine crystal seen in the exclusive resorts and convoluted glass pineapples and coconuts found in the more common tourist haunts. And the crowd in this particular bar…definitely not tourist. Not a camera in the bunch. To Erin, this looked like a local establishment that was well past its prime. Good-natured, well used, much appreciated. Judging from the expressions on the faces of the people enjoying their drinks, enjoying the music, enjoying the conversation, the ambiance didn't matter but the camaraderie did. She liked that, liked everything about this area so far. Except…the bartender.

"Do you know who he is?" she persisted with the man. He still ignored her. Didn't even pretend he was going to turn back round to talk to her. In fact, it seemed he was going out of his way to snub her. Maybe because she was a stranger? Or he thought her an unescorted female looking for some *action*? She didn't know, and the reason didn't really matter because he was doing it quite handily, keeping his attention fixed on wiping a single water spot off a clunky beer mug.

But Erin wasn't to be thwarted. Time truly was of the essence here. "I said—"

"I heard what you said the first time," he replied, twisting part way round then taking one dismissive, downward glance at her. "The thing is, in case you didn't notice, I don't have a sign hung out front saying tourist information." He turned his back on her and refocused on that very same spot.

"So, what happened to that Jamaican hospitality you're known for? This is supposed to be one of the friendly places in the world. You know, people with impeccable manners, good ethics."

"Are you talking about this bar, specifically?" he asked. "Because I don't recall reading that in any of the island literature."

"All I wanted was to find out if you know Adam Coulson. It's a simple request. I'm willing to pay for the information." Erin plunked two one-thousand-dollar Jamaican notes down on the bar, the equivalent of about twenty-two

American dollars or a little over fourteen British pounds. "Is that enough to buy an answer?" Her Realtor had told her to come to Trinique's and ask. This was Trinique's, she was asking. So far, though, she wasn't getting what she wanted.

The bartender turned round, pocketed the money in one swift movement, then said, "Yes."

"Yes, what?"

"Yes, I know Adam Coulson."

"And?"

"And that's what you asked, that's what you paid for. I answered your question, the deal is over."

"Meaning you want more money?"

"No. Two thousand was enough. And I appreciate it since I didn't have to work hard for it." He smiled, gave her a fake salute. Picked up another glass and started to polish.

Erin wasn't going to be deterred by this man. Six months...she'd been working toward this for six months and nothing was going to stop her. *Nothing!* Time was precious now. Her father was going blind, slowly but surely. Being put off by the bartender, or by Dr Adam Coulson, wasn't an option. "Well, I *don't* appreciate it. You knew exactly what I wanted, and you took advantage of me." She held out her hand, palm up. "Give it back. Or tell me where I can find Adam Coulson."

He studied her for a moment, like he was weighing his options. Then he turned his back on her yet again and continued polishing. In the background, the Jamaican singer, a happy-looking young man with dreadlocks halfway down to his waist and a smile that nearly offset the bartender's bad mood raised the level of the steel drums he was playing, causing the dozen or so people sitting at the tiny two-tops scattered around the open-style hut to raise the level of their talking.

This was a waste of time. A complete, absurd waste of time. And while so far, every islander she'd met had been friendly, this bartender, who was obviously *not* an islander, was the first one she'd met who was disagreeable. More than disagreeable, he was downright hostile. There was no point talking to him. She'd have to get her information elsewhere.

Without another word, Erin Glover spun around and marched out of Trinique's, not so much angry over losing her money but over the fact that she'd been gullible, that she'd been taken advantage of. Her father had taught her better, had taught her how to get along in the world, no matter what the situation. She could almost see him laughing at her…good-naturedly. Laughing, and teaching her another life lesson… *Don't be so naive, Erin. People out there are always waiting for your kind.*

Algernon Glover. Drs Algernon and Erin Glover. Adoptive father and daughter. They were an odd pairing to be sure. Full-blooded Jamaican father, full-blooded Irish daughter. As her father always said, *the black and white of it.* Some people considered it a pairing to stare at, but she considered it…normal. She'd met her father when she'd been five, and he'd saved her life many times since then, in both the literal as well as the emotional sense. She loved the man dearly, owed him everything she was and everything she had, and she wasn't going to let one dimwit bartender stand in her way.

"He's the one you want."

Erin turned back to the door. "Who?"

"I heard the conversation. Saw the way he treated you. Shameful. But he's got a lot on his mind these days, and he's regretting his decision to sell his land."

It was the singer. From a distance he looked older. Up close, he looked twenty, give or take a year. Decked out in rust-colored and blue-striped cotton pants and a white cotton shirt, he was simply standing there, waiting to give her information. And not holding out his hand for a gratuity. "I'm not sure I understand," she said, trying to exercise the caution her father had taught her.

"Adam Coulson. He's the one you want. You're the doctor who wants to buy his land, aren't you? Dr Glover? We got word from Port Wallace a while ago that you were coming here, looking for him."

"Actually, I'm the one who already bought his land." She was amazed how quick the news of her arrival had spread. She'd made the enquiries and word of her trip up to Regina had raced here faster than she could have gotten there.

"Well, that's him." He pointed to the bartender. "Over there. The one baring his teeth and growling like an angry dog."

"Can't be. The Adam Coulson I want to talk to is the local doctor. That guy looks more like the local malcontent."

"One's not exclusive of the other, you know. And that's Adam Coulson, the full-time doctor and part-time malcontent." He held out his hand to Erin. "I'm Davion Thomas, by the way. On my good days, I'm a singer here at Trinique's. On my best days, I'm a future medical school student and a current paramedic being employed by Adam Coulson… the doctor, not the malcontent." He pointed to the bartender again. "Him."

"So when I asked him, why didn't he tell me who he was?"

"Like I said, you're the one who bought his property and he's not fond of you because of that. He's also having second thoughts."

Erin blinked twice. "So I'm the bad guy here because I bought what he offered for sale?"

"Apparently, you are. And I'd like to tell you that he'll get over it, but Adam's a strong man with strong opinions. It could take him a while."

"So, in the mean time, while I'm waiting for him to get over his strong opinion, I'm supposed to do what?"

Davion shrugged. "Stay out of his way, maybe. Let him adjust."

"I don't have time to stay out of his way. I'm here to complete the business transaction for *my* property."

"Your property, his dreams. He'll adjust, but you being here in person has set him off. He's having a hard time reconciling to those dreams disappearing. That's why he's so…"

She knew what it was like to lose a dream and she did feel bad for him in that. But business was business, and she was on a timeline. "That's why he's being so grumpy," she supplied. Watching him for a moment, she noticed that he was quite obviously avoiding looking at her. Going out of his way, in fact, to dodge eye contact. So much so it was obvious to anyone who cared to consider the dynamics. "So, he's the doctor *and* the bartender?" Odd combination. In med school, many of her friends had held a variety of jobs to make their way through, but by the time they'd started to practice, most of those jobs had been discarded.

Davion stepped a little closer to Erin. Not so much as to be offensive but more like he was about to reveal a secret he didn't want overheard. "He's not the bartender, but he steps in when he's asked to. He *is* the doctor, though, like I said. Treats everyone in Regina and all the area around it when they need medical attention. He's a good man, Dr Glover. Takes care of us, never turns anybody away when they can't pay, and most of the time they can't pay. But he doesn't want to get *involved* with people so much."

Surprisingly, she had a flash of admiration for Coulson for what he did as a doctor. But as quickly as it had come, one look at his scowl and it vanished. "Look, I'm glad he has a good medical ethic, but that has nothing to do with me. All I want here is to get the deed to my property and be done with this."

"Except he doesn't want to sell it to you now."

"But he already sold it. And took my money." She liked Davion. He had a real charm about him, and a maturity well beyond his years. But as nice as Davion was, she would have preferred to have this conversation with Adam Coulson himself.

Davion shrugged. "I think sometimes he gets worried. Tries to figure out how he's going to keep the clinic open. People here get sick like they do everyplace else, but they don't have very much to pay him, so he's limited in what he can do. Mostly, he's the one who supports his clinic, and times are tough for him."

This was more than she wanted to know. Davion was telling her things that, quite frankly, she wasn't interested in. All she wanted was her medical complex—one main hospital building, a dozen outbuildings of various sizes. Near a beach. That last was the part she wanted the most. Her dream. Her father's dream. *When I can't see any longer, I want to hear...the laughter of children, the sounds of the ocean...* "Look, I need to talk to him, but it's pretty clear he's not going to talk to me. So, can you tell me where his clinic is? Maybe I can go there and wait until he's finished with his job here."

"He won't be off until closing time. Three in the morning. And his clinic...I don't think he has plans to go there today. Right now, people come here to Trinique's to see him."

Well, this was going nowhere and her aggravation level was ballooning. "Three o'clock?"

"Maybe a little later, if he stays to clean up. Usually, he does that the next morning, though."

Erin glanced at her watch. "Fine, I'll wait for him."

"He's not very friendly after a long shift at the bar."

"He's not very friendly now, so what difference does it make?"

Davion grinned. "More than you know, Dr Glover."

She looked back over at Coulson for a moment, caught his eye. Saw…anger. But why was he taking this would-be business transaction so personally? Hating her for no apparent reason? That's what she saw in that brief glance, though, before he turned away from her again. It didn't make sense to her. None of it did. "Well, I'll be back. Will you give him that message for me? I'll be back, and I'll keep coming back until he hands me my deed."

"That could be a while. He's pretty stubborn. In the meantime, have you got a place to stay?" Davion looked at her bags, sitting in the sand next to the door.

"Not yet. But I saw a couple of places back up the road, about an hour's drive." She'd hoped to stay in one of the cottages she supposedly owned, but that wasn't working out, so far. "Or I can go back to one of the larger towns." Port Wallace perhaps. It was not a tourist spot, but nice. Two hours away on a bumpy road, though, which wasn't going to improve her disposition.

"You can stay here, at Trinique's."

"In the bar?" It wasn't an offer she'd expected, but she was tempted since this trip wasn't about her comfort or convenience.

He pointed to a little cottage sitting several hundred

yards off the road. It was nearly hidden by palm trees. "That's my mother's house. She's not here now. Won't be back for several days, maybe longer. The place is empty, so if you'd like to stay there…"

Now, this was the hospitality her father had always spoken of. The Jamaica he loved, and the Jamaica she'd come to love through him. They'd traveled here often enough while she'd been growing up, to visit her grandmother Glover. This was the first time, though, she'd come without her father. The first time she wasn't here as a tourist but as someone who would eventually live here, maybe spend the rest of her life here. And the idea of staying at Trinique's cottage made her feel welcome. Certainly more welcome than Adam Coulson did. "If you don't think she'd mind…"

"My mother would mind if you didn't stay there. You're part of us now. We take care of our own."

Erin smiled brightly at the thought of belonging. It was something she never took for granted. "Then I accept. Thank you. And, please, tell your mother thank you when you talk to her." She took one last look at Adam Coulson before she went to settle in. His back was still to her and he was…studying her in the reflection of the glass he'd just polished. She waved at him, and spun away just as the sound of shattering glass quieted the bar for a moment.

Pulling another thousand-dollar note from her pocket, she handed it to Davion. "Give this to the doctor. I waited tables when I was in medical school, and we always had to pay for the dishes we broke. Tell him that glass he just dropped was on me!"

"You told her?" Adam growled at Davion. "Why the hell did you do that?" He sat down on the step into Trinique's and handed a bottle of soda to the young boy who sat down next to him. Tadeo. Aged eight. His shadow a good bit of the time.

"Because it was the right thing to do, and you know that. She made a long trip to come see you, to finish the business deal you started, and you owe her an explanation. Or her money back."

"What I owe her is…nothing."

"Nothing," Tadeo parroted, assuming a scowl like Adam's.

"See, even Tadeo agrees with me. And it's not like I'm going to keep her money. As soon as I have time to go to the bank in Port Wallace, I'll have it transferred back to her. Then the deal will be over with." Even though having that money was tempting him in ways he detested being tempted.

Davion pulled a stool outside and sat down. "It's not right, and you know that." He glanced at Tadeo. "And don't you go siding with Adam, you hear? Because Adam has to do the right thing."

"He will," Tadeo defended. "He'll do the right thing."

"Yes, he will, because he is trying to set a good example for you, Tadeo." Davion grinned at Adam then took a swig of his own soda.

"Are you two ganging up on me?" Adam grumbled.

"For your own good," Davion said. "Backing out on that deal isn't right, and you know it."

"A lot of things aren't right. If I bothered myself worrying about all of them I'd never be able to drag myself from job to job."

"OK, I get your point. You don't want to be bothered with her. But did you see that red hair on her?"

Adam had. And he'd rather liked it. Lots of red hair… red, the color of an old penny. And wild, like the wind had swept through it once and decided to stay there. "What about her hair?"

"She's going to be stubborn. One look at her, and you can tell she's not going to give up. And you, Adam, are her target. Like it or not, you're going to have to deal with her. Sooner, not later." He grinned. "Which is why I gave her directions to your cottage. You need to get it over with, and quit being so miserable. You're scaring the kiddies who come to the clinic. Even Tadeo's looking a little worried."

Adam regarded the boy at his side. No parents, and his mother's cousin was raising him now. But he was neglected. Or more like overlooked. And he was so eager to please, eager to help. The son he would have, if he could. "You're not worried about me, are you?"

"Some," Tadeo said without hesitation. "You're grumpy lately. Sometimes it scares me that maybe you don't like me any more."

Now, that made Adam feel truly terrible. He loved this kid. Tadeo had wormed his way into a special place in Adam's heart and there was no way he wanted him to feel like that. "You know you're my best friend, don't you?" He tousled Tadeo's scraggly black hair. "That's not going to change, even when I'm grumpy."

"Best friend," Tadeo said, holding up his hand to high-five him.

"For ever," Adam said, as their hands slapped.

"Now, maybe you should go high-five Dr Glover," Davion suggested.

"Well, maybe I would, except, I've got to get back to work." He stood. "And, Tadeo, come back later and we'll have dinner together, if Pabla doesn't mind." Pabla Reyes, Tadeo's guardian, never minded. "Conch fritters OK with you?"

Tadeo gave him a thumbs-up, handed Adam the empty soda bottle, then dashed off toward the beach.

"He needs better," Davion said.

"At least we agree on something," Adam responded on his way back to the bar. He worried about Tadeo, worried about Davion, too, but in a different way. Davion's mother was Trinique, a salt-of-the earth kind of woman who had raised her son in the best possible way. She was saving to send Davion to medical school, and Davion was saving, too. But times were tough, and at the rate they were going, Davion's medical education was a long way off. But with the money from the sale of his property, Adam was going to be able to help get Davion there sooner. Which was why, ultimately, he would turn over the deed to his property. He knew that, even though he couldn't bring himself to admit it. His clinic needed supplies. He was out of all but a few of the necessary drugs, he needed a new stethoscope… couldn't afford even the damned wooden tongue depressors, which were cheap. More than anything, though, the world needed the likes of Davion Thomas as a doctor.

Selling his little piece of land was going to make it all possible. Like it or not, he'd do the right thing by Dr Glover, because he had to. But he was still going to be grumpy for a while. He deserved that much.

"I know that look on your face," Davion said, stepping up to the bar.

"There's no look on my face."

"Sure there is." Davion grinned. "Look in the mirror, see it for yourself. It's the look that says you're going to give the property deed to Dr Glover and be nice to your new neighbor."

"I might be thinking about finishing *Stella*, and selling her."

"Ah, but you love that boat too much. You'd never sell

her. Not even if you had to sell the both halves of your property instead of just one."

He was correct in that assumption. That boat was a huge connection to his past, to his grandfather. It was the one thing in his life he'd never part with. "OK, if she's there when I get home, I'll talk to her. I'll give her the deed then tell her to leave me the hell alone. There, does that make you happy?"

"Or she'll tell you to leave *her* the hell alone. She's a strong woman, Adam. Like my mother. Once they know what they want, they don't let anything stand in their way, and you've been standing in Dr Glover's way."

"I'm not even going to get into a conversation with you about strong women, Davion. You know how I feel on *that* subject." His ex-wife had been a strong woman and look how that had turned out for him. Now strong women made him run in the opposite direction. He just didn't have it in him to deal with them any more. Not that there'd really been a woman since…he wasn't going to think about that discouraging part of his life since there hadn't been a woman beating a path to his door since he'd settled here permanently.

"Well, the strong lady in question won't be waiting for you at your house. She's staying at my mother's."

"You asked her to stay here?" He swiped an angry hand through his hair. "Meaning she's there right now, probably getting ready to waylay me on the way out the door when I get off work tonight."

Davion grinned. "Probably. But you have it coming."

"Whose side are you on?"

"I just want everybody to be happy."

"And what, in all this, is going to make *me* happy?"

"The medicine you can buy for your clinic. You know

it will. And I wouldn't mind a new otoscope for the clinic to make me a little happier, if that counts for anything."

"It counts." Point made. It was hard being grumpy around Davion, even when Adam wanted to be grumpy, because Davion radiated happiness and enthusiasm. He never, ever saw the negative in any situation. "So, I'll try and be happy. And I'll even apologize to the lady. But I get the feeling that an apology won't be enough for her. She's going to want a pound of my flesh, too." He looked out the window across from the bar, saw Erin Glover standing on Trinique's front porch, leaning against the white column, arms folded tightly across her chest. It was breezy, her hair was blowing. Dressed in a gauzy skirt and a tank top, she was…well, unfortunately she was just about the sexiest thing he'd ever laid eyes on. Which was a problem because the last sexy thing he'd got himself tangled up with had taken him for a ride that, even after two years past its legal end, still stung. "And in the meantime, I'm going to wait on customers for the next several hours and make sure you study those medical books I gave you. Jamaica itself may not have a recognized paramedic program, but I've got pretty tough standards for *my* paramedic. If you expect to stay working for me, you've got to keep cracking those books." Actually, that's what Davion did in every spare minute he had. He studied harder than Adam had ever studied in medical school. Which was why Davion was going to be a great doctor. He was motivated. He had passion. And he was smart.

Davion rolled his eyes, then retreated to the rear corner of Trinique's, where he had a table set up with all his books and study materials. When he wasn't working in the clinic, he spent his days and nights studying part of the time and singing the rest of the time. It was his soulful voice that brought in the customers, and it was his soul that would make him a great doctor someday. Adam wanted to be part of that, part of something good, because good hadn't really touched his life in a long, long time.

For a moment, his attention wandered back to the front porch of Trinique's cottage, where Erin Glover was still standing, still looking rigid. Then he meandered down to the end of the bar to wait on a customer, trying to forget the image that just didn't want to let go.

CHAPTER TWO

"It looks bad. Is Trinique here?"

The man standing in front of Erin was holding a child in his arms. A child with a foot wrapped in a bloody towel. Instantly, Erin wanted to see the wound. "Bring him into the house," she instructed, pushing open the door.

"We want to see Trinique."

"I'm sorry, but she's not here. Davion said she would be gone for a while."

"Then I have to go see Doc Adam. He'll know what to do."

"Is Trinique a doctor?" Erin asked, clearly confused.

"No, ma'am. But she's been taking care of us for a long time. Before Doc Adam, and since he's working at the bar today, I didn't want to bother him."

"Look, I'm a doctor. I take care of children. Could I have a look at your son's foot? See what I can do for him?" She wasn't prepared, really. Didn't have her medical kit. Hadn't even come here as a doctor. But a child in need... she couldn't turn them away.

The man wasn't convinced, a sentiment that shone clearly on his face. "Doc Adam will do it fine, since Trinique isn't here. But I appreciate the offer."

"Doc Adam isn't being a doctor right now. He's busy serving beer and rum," she said, instantly regretting the cutting remark. She didn't know his circumstances and he certainly didn't deserve the professional slap. "Look, how about I just take a little look? You bring your boy inside then while I get the wound cleaned up a little, you can go and get Doc Adam."

That seemed to appease the man, because he brushed right past Erin and ran straight to the daybed in the front room, where he laid his son down. "His name is Tyjon, and I'm Ennis. Ennis Clarke." He extended a hand to Erin, and shook hard when she took it. "I appreciate your offer. Good afternoon, ma'am Doctor."

Good morning. Good afternoon. Good evening. The polite, customary greeting always used when addressing others. It was expected, especially in the more rural areas such as Regina. Her father had told her about this, told her to remember it. "Good afternoon, Mr Clarke. I'll take very good care of Tyjon."

Apparently, Ennis Clarke trusted that, because he turned and ran out the door, which gave Erin only a few minutes to assess the boy's foot before Adam Coulson took over. She didn't like that idea. But, then, she had no idea what kind of doctor he was. Didn't even know if he was a real doctor, for that matter. "So, tell me what happened, Tyjon."

"I stepped on glass. Broken bottle in the street. Cut my foot."

"When? This morning?"

He shook his head. "Two days ago. It wasn't so bad then. We washed it and it was OK. But now it hurts worse. And it started to bleed some more."

She began unwrapping the towel, trying to be gentle because the dried blood had caused it to stick to his foot. When Tyjon winced, she slowed down the process, and as she peeled back the bulky layers and got closer to the wound, the smell of infection became noticeable. "Did you wash it with soap?" she asked.

He nodded. "My mother washed it very good."

"And did you put on shoes and socks after you washed it?"

"No, ma'am Doctor. I don't like shoes."

Down to the last layer, she peeled it back carefully, and what she found wasn't good. The cut was on his heel, almost the length of his heel. Very jagged, very dirty. And swollen. There was also pus, much more than she'd expected. General redness everywhere. On top of that, his whole foot seemed warm and slightly puffy. She needed supplies, something antiseptic to start the cleaning. Antibiotics at the very least. Suture materials. But she had…nothing at all.

Erin looked around. If Trinique was a healer of some kind, maybe she had a first aid kit. "I'll be right back, Tyjon. I need to go and find something to clean up your foot."

Water would work for starters. Get the dirt off. Give her a better look at what she had to deal with.

In the kitchen, she filled a basin full of water, grabbed two clean dishtowels then returned to Tyjon, who was laughing over something Doc Adam had apparently told him. Adam Coulson looked up at her. Saw the basin of water. "Fetching my cleaning supplies for me?" he asked.

"What I'm fetching is a basin of water so I can begin to clean Tyjon's foot."

"She's a ma'am doctor," Ennis Clarke explained quite seriously.

"So she says," Adam snorted, standing then walking straight over to Erin and taking the basin of water from her hands. "My bag…" He pointed to it sitting next to the door. "Find my antibiotic cream in there. If I have any left. And

I probably have some suture. See if you can also come up with a vial of lidocaine, too. I'm pretty sure I have some of that."

"Pretty sure?"

He shrugged. "Supplies aren't easy to come by. We have to make do, sometimes."

"How do you make do without suture? Or lidocaine?" Lidocaine hydrochloride, more specifically, was the anesthetic agent he'd inject into Tyjon to dull the pain of the stitches.

"When you don't have it, you don't have it. So, you improvise."

She wasn't sure what that meant. Wasn't sure she even wanted to find out.

"Davion," Adam continued, "run back to the clinic and see if I have any antibiotic cream samples there so I can give them to Ennis. I think I might have a few left. Also, bring me a syringe and a vial of penicillin."

"Penicillin?" Nobody used that any more. There were newer, much more effective drugs on the market. Occasionally, she'd prescribed one of the penicillin derivatives, but never penicillin itself.

"Good drug," Adam quipped. "Highly underrated today, and even more highly underused."

"And cheap," Davion said on his way out the door.

"Well, that, too," Adam agreed. He dipped the kitchen towel into the basin of water and started to wash Tyjon's foot.

It had to hurt. She saw the poor boy grimacing, and wondered if the infection had spread beyond his foot. What she saw even more than that, though, was the gentle way Coulson was taking care of Tyjon. Soothing hands. It was a term her father used. He'd always said the best doctors didn't get so tied up in the book learning that they forgot how to have soothing hands. He'd had those soothing hands for her all those times she'd been sick after her chemotherapy, during all those times she hadn't been sure if she'd live or die. She remembered her father's soothing hands and right now what she saw with Adam Coulson was what she'd known from her father.

"What can I do to help?" she asked, after a quick look through his medical bag produced a vial with barely enough lidocaine to do the job, a scant amount of fresh suture, a few pieces of candy, a package of sterile gauze strips and a stethoscope with shredded rubber earpieces.

"You a surgeon?" he asked.

She shook her head. "Pediatrician."

"Then you'd be good at stitches because kids always need them." Assumption made. It wasn't a question.

"I've done my fair share."

"OK, I'll let you do the honors. In the meantime, freshen up the water in the basin."

The water was nearly black with dirt, which made her cringe because all that dirt had come from Tyjon's foot.

"Please," Adam added.

"What?"

"Please. You were standing there, staring at the basin, so I figure you were waiting for me to say please. So… please."

She hadn't been waiting for politeness. From Adam Coulson, whom she'd known for only an hour, she expected none. But her hesitance was…well, she couldn't explain it. What she was seeing here wasn't exactly a shock, because there were areas all over the world where the medical standard was different from *her* medical standard. What she didn't understand was the doctor—his casual attitude, his lack of basic medical supplies. "Are you really a doctor?"

she asked. "Educated in a regular medical school, licensed to practice?" The question just popped out of her.

He paused in his bathing of Tyjon's foot, looked up at her, frowned for a moment, then broke into a broad smile. "A little while ago, Davion had almost convinced me to feel guilty about refusing to hand over the deed to my land. Honestly, I *was* feeling a little bad about the way I was treating you, and fully prepared to apologize for it. Like I said, that was a little while ago. But not any more. Now, the water, please."

So, maybe she deserved that. She wasn't about to apologize for asking, but she wasn't going to take too much offense to his reaction either, because she shouldn't have challenged him that way, especially not in front of Tyjon. So, before she said something else she'd regret, Erin picked up the basin, returned to the kitchen, and dumped out the old water. As she gave the basin a quick wash with dish soap and water, she thought about why she was here, and it was too important to let these skirmishes with Adam Coulson get in her way. Make no mistake, they could get in the way if she wasn't careful. He was, after all, the local doctor. While she had all her permissions in place for the hospital, and all the legalities out of the way, having the doctor with her, rather than against her, was smart. So for now, she'd have to curb her temper. "For you, Dad," she whispered, fighting the tears welling up in her eyes when she thought about the graceful way her father was accepting his fate. She didn't have that same gracefulness about her in any sense, no matter how hard she'd tried to find it within herself. She was reactionary, quick to fight. On the verge of dumping the water on Adam Coulson, although there was no grace in that. However, the thought of it did come with some surprising satisfaction. This wasn't about her, though. When she remembered that, everything else faded away.

"You crying?" Adam asked from the doorway.

"No!" she snapped, blinking hard then brushing the back of her forearm across her eyes. "I splashed soap in my eyes."

"'If thine eye offends thee, pluck it out.'"

"What?" she sputtered, spinning to face him.

"That's the kind of thing you'd expect me to say, isn't it? I don't have antibiotic cream, I still use penicillin, I make do with what I can find."

"And the rubber earpieces for your stethoscope are wearing through."

"You've judged me on several criteria that have nothing to do with my abilities as a doctor, so I thought telling you what to do with the soap in your eyes is what you'd expect from me. Especially since you haven't seen my diploma from Harvard so you don't know if I'm a real medical doctor."

"Harvard?"

He chuckled. "Preconceptions are dangerous, Dr Glover. They can get you into all kinds of trouble. So much so that you'll end up without antibiotic cream, decent rubber earpieces and a whole lot more trouble than you'd ever bargained for. Oh, and for your information, even though it's none of your business, I'd use penicillin even if something out there was cheaper, because I *like* penicillin. Now, my water?"

The strains of the music wafted over to Trinique's home, and Erin was finding herself strangely addicted to it already. It was calming. And happy. It transported her to the Jamaica her father had always told her of, the one she believed, with all her heart, was still there. Untouched.

"I wish you'd come with me," she said over the phone. "Regina is a beautiful village. The cottages…they're painted with all different colors. Reds, blues, pastels like pink and yellow. Every one a different combination. And they've all got so many types of tropical flowers in the yards… It's like an artist's pallet. Then, the people…they're so nice. They just take you in and treat you like you belong, like you're part of their family. Well, all but one, and he doesn't count since he's not Jamaican." She wasn't about to tell her father of the trouble brewing with the land purchase. As far as he knew, she had the deed by now and everything was moving forward. Oh, she was pretty sure Coulson would turn it over, but it was going to be in his own good time. Which wasn't her time, as she had her dad fully involved now in the business plans for the new hospital, and the sooner those were finalized, the sooner he'd come to Jamaica… she hoped. It was her intention to put him in charge of the hospital, blind or not. Algernon Glover, Chief of Staff at the Algernon Glover Hospital. Maybe it would give him back some of his life. Maybe it would entice him to come out of his dark study, where he kept the shades drawn and the door closed. That's the way he lived these days and it scared her. But soon, very soon, that would be over with. She hoped. "So, why don't you come down? You can do everything you need to from here."

"I'm fine where I am, and I have more than enough to keep me busy here."

It was clear he didn't like getting too far away from his comfort zone. That, more than anything else, was what made her feel sad. She and her dad had traveled to so many places together over the years, and done so many things. "But you could use a nice holiday, and the beach here is beautiful. Nicer than anything else I've seen in Jamaica. So pristine. No tourists."

"There'll be time enough for that in a while. Right how, I still have work to do *right where I am*. And who knows? Maybe you'll find some time for a short holiday yourself. You wouldn't want your father on your arm for that, would you? Especially if you meet a nice young man who's in the mood for a little holiday, too?"

He lived in perpetual hope of that. Wanted grandchildren. But she'd…she'd never been that interested. It had been more than fifteen years since her last recurrence of leukemia, and the doctors had long since declared her recovered. Years and years of fighting the disease and all its nasty comebacks had taught her to be cautious. It had also taught her to stay focused on her goal…get through college, get through medical school, now this. Her life hadn't afforded her the luxury of having more than one goal at a time because there had been so many times when even a single goal had been a struggle. So now she had a single goal to achieve, the most important one of her life, and she wouldn't allow herself to think in terms of anything more.

"Dad, you know I'm not looking right now," she told him.

"One of my big regrets, Erin, is that I have raised such a serious daughter. You were brought up in an old man's world, I'm afraid, and you don't know how to have fun."

Her father was older, yes. But fun…her life had been filled with fun, filled with so many wonderful things. And this was her father's standard argument, the one he used to make her feel guilty. "It's not going to work," she teased.

"What's not going to work?" he asked, laughter just on the edge of his voice.

"You know what I'm talking about. And there'll be plenty of time for grandchildren, if I ever do find the right man."

"If you ever start looking."

Oh, she'd looked. Come close to finding, actually. Then been jilted because a slight illness had brought up a cancer scare, which had scared a man she might have been serious about right out the door. And he had run so hard and fast he hadn't even made the promise that he'd call, or see her again, or they'd work it out. He'd told her he loved her one week, then bolted the next. Like her high school sweetheart had when the cancer actually had returned. Or her childhood best friend had when the chemotherapy had claimed her hair. *Oh, gross, Erin. You're, like, going bald. That's so disgusting.* So, no more looking, no more expectations. Emotionally, it was easier that way. "On that note, I'm going to say goodnight. Love you, Dad."

"Love you, too, Erin. Even if you are stubborn and too serious for your own good."

He clicked off before she could get to her next comeback. And for a while after the phone call she sat with her feet propped up on the porch rail, enjoying the gentle, hot breeze, still listening to the strains of happy music wafting in. Thinking of Adam Coulson, not of her dad. Harvard education and without a decent stethoscope. On impulse, she dialed her dad back. "One more thing," she said. "Could you send me a stethoscope?"

It was a small gesture, and she kept telling herself that it was for Tyjon, and anybody else needing treatment here. Not for Coulson.

"So, let's just get this over with." A voice came at her from out of the dark a while later.

Startled by Coulson's intrusion into her pleasant solitude, Erin jumped. "Do you always sneak up on people that way?"

"I wasn't sneaking."

"And you didn't exactly announce yourself either, did you?"

"Actually, I did. I said, 'Let's just get this over with.'"

Straightening in the chair and pulling her feet off the porch rail, she was a little sad to have her evening ended so abruptly. It was nice to relax for a while. The ambiance suited her, made her feel mellow. Lately, she hadn't had time to relax, and who knew how long it had been since she'd felt mellow. "I agree," she said, standing. "Let's get this over with. Do you have my deed?"

He handed it over, without saying a word.

She didn't look at it, though. He wouldn't cheat her on this, and to look would be to insult him. No need to do that. No need to rub salt in what was obviously a very open, very raw wound. "Thank you," she said, tucking the paper into her pocket.

"Just like that," he said, almost under his breath.

"Like what?"

"Like in a split second, it's gone." He shrugged. "So that makes us neighbors now, doesn't it?"

"In proximity, yes, I suppose it does. But we don't have to be neighborly. I know you didn't want to sell your land, and I know you resent me for buying it. So it's OK with me if we're not friends, not even neighbors who wave."

"And you think that makes it better for me?"

"I don't know what makes it better for you, Coulson. I'm just making an offer. I'll stay away from you, leave you alone, won't even come to Trinique's, if it's better for you that way." It wasn't much of a gesture, considering the circumstances. But it was the best she could do.

"What's better for me is getting my property back, but that's not going to happen. You need it for whatever reason you may have, and I wanted it for whatever reason I had.

But in the end, my reason wasn't going to happen. Don't know if yours will or not."

"What was your reason?" she asked him.

"To use it as it was intended…as a hospital. But as you can see, I barely manage a clinic, so the hospital was a…"

"A dream?"

"A long way off. Money talks. You had it, I need it, and now one of us is happy while the other is better off. Fair trade, although I hate it to hell."

"Well, if it makes you feel any better, I'm going to open a children's hospital."

"Now, there's an impractical idea if ever I've heard one."

"You think a children's hospital is impractical?" she practically growled, she was so angry.

"Not in the right setting. Which is someplace accessible, a place people can get to easily, where they'll want to take their children. We're not accessible here. You already know that. And nobody in their right mind will bring their children to a place where the only way in or out is on a rutted road. Put the hospital someplace where people can use it. Not here!"

"But here is perfect." And her hospital wasn't going to be just any ordinary hospital. It was going to be everything she hadn't had when she'd spent so much time in various hospitals. It was going to be a place where being sick wasn't the focus, but being normal was.

"Shows what you know about setting up a hospital. At least, when I wanted to start a hospital here, I had enough sense to know that the area would support a very small general hospital. *General hospital*, not a specialty facility."

She tamped back her anger to face his challenge. With Adam Coulson, she had an idea that anger could turn into a steady diet, and she simply didn't want to bristle then strike every time they met. So now was as good a time as any to start reining herself in. Because she wasn't going anywhere. This was home. He was her shouting-distance neighbor. She didn't want the strife on a lingering basis. Gritting her teeth, she smiled up at him. "Then I guess it's up to me to prove you wrong, isn't it?"

"Or the other way around."

"Not going to happen, Coulson. I know what I'm doing."

"The thing is, so do I, and I also know it's a bad idea."

"You'll change your mind." She hoped.

"You'll change your plans."

"I don't think so." Standing her ground with him was... stimulating. It made her tingle. So much so, she took a step back from him. "Look, there's no point in arguing about it. I'm going forward with my plans, whether or not you like it, and there's nothing you can do to stop me."

"Actually, I can stand back and watch you fail, then buy back my property for a fraction of what you paid me for it."

He said it with a grin on his face, but she knew he was serious. The truth of the matter was, she didn't blame him. Were she in his position, she'd probably be rooting for his failure. In a way, Erin respected his resolve. Too bad they both couldn't have what they wanted. But that wasn't going to happen. For her to win, he had to lose. For him to win, she had to lose, and that was something she just wasn't going to do. The only thing was, he didn't know how much she needed this hospital, how much she had to make the idea work. "Look, I don't want to keep arguing, OK? We're not going to agree, we might not even get along very well. But we're going to be neighbors, and because of that I'd like to try for some civility between us. Even if it's just civility on the surface for the sake of appearances."

"So we smile and bare our fangs when we pass each other, and make sure we growl under our breath?"

She couldn't help but laugh at him. The man did have his charm. It was coarse, and quite deviant, but she rather liked it. "Look, what can I do to smooth a little bit of the bumpy road between us so I don't always have to bare my fangs? It causes wrinkles."

"Funny you should ask, because I expect I'll be seeing at least fifteen patients first thing in the morning at the clinic. That's the usual number. I've promised Trinique three more days at the bar…she's visiting her sick sister in Miami. And in between serving drinks I'll see at least another dozen or so patients…in the back room. Trinique had it set up as a small clinic for me. Oh, and work until about three, when the bar closes. Meaning my days are getting pretty long. So, if you're serious about your offer, I could use your help at the clinic. Then that way you can see where the real medical need is here."

Honestly, his schedule surprised her. She'd pictured him more the hardly working type than the working hard type. "Do you work like that every day?" she asked, not really intending to seem so interested.

"No, sometimes I have more patients than that. You know, make a few house calls. Go up to Fontaine and squeeze in house calls there. Tomorrow seems a little light, which is why it's probably the best day this week to have you see why general medical care is what the area needs."

"Always plotting, aren't you, Coulson?"

"I'd rather think of it as moving forward."

She thought for a moment. Right now, there wasn't much for her to do. She wouldn't be meeting with her architects for a couple of days, and her plans were already far enough along that at this point there really wasn't a whole lot more to work on. So, why not? Getting to know the people here was a good idea because she was going to be one of them, and what better way to do it than working in the clinic? Admittedly, she missed working. Somewhere over the past weeks it had taken a backseat to her hospital, so much so that she'd finally left her practice. She missed it, and this would help ease the dull ache that had been settling in. In her heart she was a doctor, and that's what she needed to be doing. Adam Coulson might think he was handing her part of his plan for her failure, but she looked at it as just the opposite. "OK, I'll work in the clinic."

"You will?"

She stood to face him, drew every bit of her five feet eight inches up to his well-over-six-foot physique, and stared him straight in the eye. "Just tell me what time, and I'll be there." In the light from the single yellow bulb dangling on the other side of the porch, he was just about the best-looking man she'd ever seen. She'd looked from afar earlier, and had totally missed the detail in his eyes. The kindness there. The twinkling. Normally, she didn't look at men this way and right now it bothered her that she was enjoying her long, rather cheeky look at him. Enjoying it too much. So she took another step backward, then two more just to be on the safe side. "But here's the deal. For every day I work for you I expect a day in return where you won't be plotting my demise...at least, where I can see it so obviously."

"You drive a hard bargain, Red."

"I'm offering you free labor, Coulson. You want me to see the real medical need here in the hope that I'll back off? This is the only way it's going to happen."

"Then a day for a day it is."

He held out his hand to shake on the deal, and when she took it, the jolt that passed between them passed all the way down to her toes. Did he feel it? She couldn't tell by the expression on his face, but it was so real he had to. Or, maybe her imagination was simply getting away from her, being in a tropical paradise with a handsome man, and all. Whatever it was, she allowed the handshake to linger but a moment then pulled her hand back. Put up her imaginative safety net. "Tomorrow morning, Coulson."

"Tomorrow morning…Red."

The walk was short from Trinique's cottage, down a long, winding jungle path, and each of her steps was deliberately slow. Sure, she'd seen the hospital compound online, knew the look of the buildings by heart. But there was a world of difference between the internet and in person, and she was actually a little nervous about this. She'd done it. She had her property—one hospital building, a handful of small cottages, and a stretch of beach. Paradise in a way most people would define it.

"He's very grumpy this morning," Davion said, catching up to her then falling into step. "When he came back to the bar last night, he broke glasses…on purpose. Threw a couple on the floor then took the money you'd given him earlier and put it into the cash register for my mother."

She pulled the deed from the pocket of her skirt for Davion to see. "He didn't give in without a fight. I know it wasn't easy for him."

"But he always does the right thing. Sometimes it takes him a while but, like I told you before, he's a good man."

"I think he's a very…interesting man."

Davion nodded. "That, too. And stubborn."

"I've definitely seen that side of him."

"And he's seen that side of you, hasn't he?"

"How did you get to be so perceptive at your age?"

Davion chuckled. "Being around Adam. He's been in and out of half my life now, and I've been learning from the master."

"Well, that's what's going to make you an exceptional doctor. You know how to read people. So, you say he's been in and out of your life for most of your life. How long, exactly, has he been here?"

"Off and on, almost twelve years, I guess. Started coming when he was in medical school, came more often when he was out. Until he moved here permanently a couple of years ago."

Well, she couldn't fault Coulson for that. Jamaica was a wonderful place to visit. She'd been coming here almost from the day her father had adopted her, nearly twenty-five years ago. He'd bring her when she was well, and she'd feel guilty when she was sick because she knew she was keeping him from coming.

"So, is this your first time to the island, Dr Glover?"

"Please, call me Erin. And no. I've been here so many times I can't remember. My father was from here…and my grandmother lived here until her dying day. Almost as far back as I can remember we tried to get here at least three or four times a year, more often if we could."

"And where would here be, if I may ask?"

"In her later years, my grandmother moved to Kingston because of her health. But when she was young she lived in Alligator Pond. Ran a little fishing industry there, had a couple of boats." That was being modest. Her grandmother had been a major player in the fishing business there, a woman well respected in her industry.

Davion arched his eyebrows. "Alligator Pond doesn't have many…*redheads*."

Erin laughed. "My grandmother wasn't a redhead. Have you ever heard of Odessia Glover?"

Davion gave a soft whistle. "She was an honorable lady, well known for her generosity. She was your grandmother?"

Nodding, Erin added, "And Algernon Glover is my father."

"A respected gentleman. I'm impressed. Surprised, but impressed."

"I was impressed, too, the first time I met him. And after all these years, he still impresses me." She stopped, looked ahead, held her breath. "Is that my hospital?"

"That's it. And all those buildings to the north. Adam told me that he's put up a dividing line, and you're not to cross over it. That everything on the other side is private property."

"The rope?" She had to laugh. There was a slack rope tied loosely from palm tree to palm tree—in places it dipped into the sand. A lame, funny gesture, actually.

"I told you he's stubborn. And if you haven't looked at your bill of sale at the back of the deed he gave you last night, he's added a provision on the end of it."

She pulled the paper from her pocket, thumbed through the few pages and, sure enough, he'd penciled it in. A fence? "How like him!"

"Good fences make good neighbors!" Adam shouted, stepping out from a copse of palms. His side of the line, of course.

She jumped. "Why do you sneak up on people that way?"

"Why are you always so jumpy?"

"Look, I've got to go," Davion said. "I'm helping in the clinic this morning and the patients are probably already lining up. They heard there's a lady doctor here and they want to see her." With that, he trotted off, crossed under the rope, and headed toward the larger of three buildings she could see on the other side of Coulson's group of palm trees.

Erin strolled over to the dividing line, but didn't cross it. "Are you serious about the fence?" she asked him.

His answer was a grin and a shrug. "Just trying to keep things honest between us."

"It's a rope, Coulson. Not even a taut rope."

"A fence by any other name…"

"And how do I know this so-called fence is the true dividing line? Maybe it's well over on my side and you're cheating me of something I rightfully own."

"What you rightfully own, Red, are the buildings, and the easement all the way down to the beach. I was being generous, giving you this little strip along the side here, because I thought, at some point, you might like to put in a better drive up to the hospital's front door. But I could take it back, if you don't want it."

"And what do you want in additional payment, Doctor? A case of glasses to smash?"

"Stubborn, and with a temper, too. You're actually pretty cute when you're acting like that. It sets off the sparks in your green eyes."

"Hazel. Not green." She gave in to him with a laugh. "So, is this how the neighbor relationship is going to work between us? We're going to stand back and spar at each other from across the…rope?"

"Unless you want to build a real fence. Doesn't have to be a tall fence. Maybe six or eight feet."

So, what was it about Adam Coulson that disarmed her? Here she was, standing on her side of this convoluted boundary he'd strung up, arguing almost into a seduction with him. It wasn't that she wanted to be seduced, wasn't that she particularly wanted to be friendly. But now they were practically face-to-face, and all she could think was how good he smelled—all masculine and tropical, maybe with a hint of lime.

"Look, I know you're enjoying yourself playing gate-keeper at your rope, but am I going to have to ask permission to cross over so I can go to work? Provided you still want me to come and work."

He swooped low, in a courtly gesture. "Permission to enter. And work." Said with a grin. "Oh, and lunch."

"Lunch?"

"You know, that meal that comes in the middle of the day?"

"You're asking me to lunch?"

"Not a date, Red. A discussion. Since you're going to be handling some of my medical load for a while…"

"Wait a minute. How did one morning at your medical clinic turn into me handling part of your medical load for a while?"

"I'm busy and it's you who's drawing them in, so it's up to you to take care of them. I just thought I'd be civilized about this and go over some of the details with you."

"I'm not taking over your practice, Coulson. Just giving you a couple hours of my time."

"A couple of hours?" He pointed to the throng of people standing around one of the cottages on his side of the line. "They're here for you, Red, and I don't think you're the kind of doctor who's going to turn them down."

She studied the people for a moment. Mostly women and children. A hard draw she couldn't refuse to see, and she hated it that he had figured her out so well, so quickly, so easily. "When you say lunch, do you mean lunch as in two chairs at the dividing line, you on your side, me on mine?"

"Well, if that's the way you'd like it, sure. Why not? But I was thinking we could go back to Trinique's, have Kaven fix us his famous jerk nyamwich, I'd suggest the chicken, and bammy strips. Best on this side of the island."

Food for the gods. Her mouth was already watering. "My father makes a good nyamwich...jerk chicken or beef, lettuce, tomato... Is Kaven's served on coco bread?"

"What good nyamwich isn't on coco bread?"

"And the bammy?"

Adam smiled. "Cassava flour and secret ingredients. He won't tell anybody what they are, but I caught him smuggling yams in one day."

"A yam bammy? That's a new one on me. Guess I could be persuaded to try it."

"So, that's a yes?"

She nodded. "That's a yes, but only for the yam bammy." She stepped under the dividing line then looked back over her shoulder at her hospital. "I have a condition, too. You give me a guided tour of my property and all its buildings. Tonight."

"That's cruel, you know."

"But who better than you? Besides, you get the fence, so I get the tour. It's only fair."

He sighed. "What's fair is you selling me back what's mine, and leaving me the hell alone."

She laughed. "As they say, all's fair in..."

"War and war."

"That's your version?"

"Not until this very moment. So, in the meantime, how long has it been since you've done an obstetrical exam? Because Breeon Edward is due anytime now."

"I'm a pediatrician," she said, following along behind him on their way to the clinic.

"That's close enough."

"Close enough? I haven't delivered a baby since medical school."

"But in the whole scheme of things you do know where babies come from?" he teased.

"Of course I know where babies come from."

"Then Breeon will be happy to see you."

"I don't know, Coulson. All this for a yam bammy?" Of course, a yam bammy was unique. But, then, so was Adam Coulson. She had an idea, though, that he was an acquired taste, the way a good bammy was. Even so, she'd stick to the bammy! It was safer.

CHAPTER THREE

THE clinic wasn't at all what she'd expected. Actually, she didn't know what she'd expected, but this wasn't it. It was sparse, just a tiny waiting room with several wooden chairs and two scantily stocked exam rooms. Basic, functional and neat. Tidy almost to perfection. Each exam room contained one exam table, a very old-fashioned type possibly fifty years out of date, one supply cabinet, a sink and a stool. There was room enough to turn around, barely enough room for much more. But the paint was fresh. White. Spotless. Everything very professional, including the white jacket Coulson handed her.

"We don't have much in the way of medical amenities here, but looking the part gives our patients more confidence in us," he said as he tugged on his knee-length white coat. "Shows respect for them, too. Like they matter enough for us to be professional."

That was almost as surprising as everything else here. It was all bare bones. The cabinets she peeked into contained almost nothing. The locked medicine cabinet he showed her had so few medications to choose from there was almost no point in locking it. And as far as instruments…there was a dearth there as well. Bare bones, yet in some strange way impressive. An admirable doctor making do with so little. "It's…"

"It's like nothing you've ever seen," he finished for her. "You probably didn't even know that medicine existed on this level, did you?"

"I'm not that sheltered," she said defensively.

He chuckled. "Sure you are. Rich doctor, probably from a rich family... You handed me a few hundred thousand dollars for ten acres of land and some buildings that, in Jamaica, is worth much less than half of that. Which tells me until this very moment you didn't know about medicine on my level."

"OK, I've had advantages, and I'm not ashamed of it. My father came from a working family who did well for themselves, and I benefited from that. But that doesn't mean I'm sheltered." Although right now she did feel that way.

"Well, sheltered or not, we've got people lining up outside, waiting to be seen. You get the women and children, I get the men." He pointed out the window to a group, all sitting in various types of plastic chairs. The ones she'd seen from afar earlier. Some were reading, a couple of the women were sewing, children were playing. Two of the men were engaged in a game of checkers. It was a casual, friendly scene.

"Then it looks like I've got my work cut out for me, because the women and children outnumber the men three to one, which means I also get Davion to assist me." She pulled on the white coat and almost drowned in it, it was so large. "Perfect fit," she said, rolling up her sleeves, and, in fact, looking forward to seeing patients.

Adam straightened the jacket's collar, his hand accidentally brushing over the line of her jaw. Goosebumps immediately leapt to her arms. "Davion's good. The future best doctor in Jamaica. So..." He held up the one stethoscope. "This is it, and the tubing is brittle. I have one blood-pressure cuff, not calibrated, and not able to be calibrated it's so old. So be gentle if you need to use them, and use them sparingly because they don't have much life left in them."

She noted the patches of tape on the stethoscope, and was glad she'd asked her dad for a new one. Next time she talked to him she was going to ask for a blood-pressure cuff and who knew what else. "The medical authority on the island doesn't provide you with any kind of assistance?" she asked.

"Assistance goes to the public hospitals and medical facilities. And those are mostly in the larger cities, serving the majority of the population base, as well as the tourists. It makes sense, to keep the medicine where the majority of the people are. Out here…we're on our own. We get lots of sympathy and emotional support from the health ministry and the rest is up to us. Overall, they're doing a fairly good job of administering health care throughout the island, especially with the limited resources they have. But there are still areas like this where medical care is hard to come by, either because the people don't want to travel to seek it out or they can't."

"So you're the equivalent of the old-fashioned country doctor, the one who goes to the patient rather than having the patient come to him."

"Something like that."

And he supported his medical practice out of his own pocket. That, if nothing else, was certainly painting a different picture of him than the one she'd originally seen. "Look, Coulson, I think I had an attitude about your working at the bar. That's before I knew…"

"It buys the penicillin," he said, shrugging. "Sometimes, you do what you have to do."

"I'm sorry about that penicillin remark, too." She took the battered stethoscope from his hand then the blood-pressure cuff. "And to show you how much, I'll buy the bammy. Now, I'm going to go see the pregnant woman first. She looks like she needs to get home and get comfortable more than anybody else here." Erin glanced out the window, watched her sitting uncomfortably in a green plastic chair, watched the way she clung to her husband's hand and the way he rubbed the small of her back with his other hand. It was nice. In a way, she envied the woman.

"First child," Adam explained. "Due in a couple of weeks, and I'm hoping you can convince her to go to one of the hospitals, because I can't. Oh, and I do have a speculum you can use to examine her. Davion will get it for you."

Thirty minutes later, after as a good an exam as Erin could give Breeon Edward, she tapped on the door of the exam room where Adam was examining an older man. "Can you step out here for a minute?" she asked, when he opened the door a crack. "There's something I need to talk to you about."

"Give me five minutes," he said.

Erin used those five minutes to try out her powers of persuasion on Breeon. "Having your baby in a hospital is a good thing because they have different ways to help you, and your baby."

Breeon shook her head. "My husband can't take me. Leron drives the bus that goes to the villages and he can't take the time off work. But that's OK. We can have the baby here, and everything will be just fine."

"What if I could find someone else to drive you to a hospital so Leron wouldn't have to take off work?"

Breeon gave her head a firm shake. "My mother is here, and my sister. The hospital won't let them help. Doc Adam can do this, and Trinique, if she gets back. And now that you're here, you can help, too, if you want. But no hospital."

That was the end of the argument. Breeon slid down off the exam table and headed to the door. "Doc Adam is checking me every two days now, so I'll see you in two days. Good morning, ma'am Doc." With that, Breeon exited, grinning from ear to ear as Leron met her in the hallway.

Only Erin wasn't grinning when she met Adam in the hallway moments later. "It's breech," she said.

"Damn," he muttered. "She's had a rough pregnancy. Carrying too much baby for her small frame. But I didn't expect this."

"Well, not only is it breech, she won't go to the hospital. Refuses."

"Did you tell her the baby's breech?"

Erin nodded. "Explained the best way I know how about what the delivery is going to be like if the baby doesn't turn back, including the possible complications to both her and the baby—umbilical cord prolapse, oxygen deprivation, neurological damage. Told her she'd be better off in a hospital where they could take all the necessary steps to make it an easier delivery, and also take care of any difficulties that might arise. But she has all the confidence in the world in you and Trinique, and she's not going to be talked out of her decision to have this baby right here. I even offered to find her a ride to a hospital since her husband can't take off work."

"Pretty much the same arguments I've been using for weeks, before the baby went breech."

"Well, maybe it will turn back. A good many of them do before the birth. And I do know of some pre-birth techniques she can use that might help that baby turn. I think I'll talk to her about them day after tomorrow, at her next appointment."

He arched his eyebrows. "You're going to be here day after tomorrow, seeing patients?"

She hadn't even thought about that. Certainly hadn't meant to commit to it. But that's exactly what she'd done and, truthfully, she was worried about Breeon. Having faith in your physician was good, but Breeon's faith overshadowed the practicality of the matter. She was going to have a difficult birth, one way or another, and this clinic wasn't set up to do an emergency Cesarean section, if that's what it came to. Wasn't set up to do any sort of emergency procedure on the baby either, and that particularly bothered her. "I suppose I could, if you need some help. Or I could just come over and talk to Breeon."

"I never refuse a volunteer. But don't expect payment in bammys for every little thing you do."

After she'd walked away, seen seven more patients and was on her way over to Trinique's for lunch, she wondered exactly what she had expected. One thing was certain. It hadn't been Adam Coulson. He was off-putting yet, in some strange way, fascinating. The truth was, she admired his dedication to something he believed in, even if that dedication was trying to maneuver itself into her path. Sure, he was hoping she'd fail so he could get his property back, and he wasn't shy about admitting that. But he wasn't really wishing her ill, doing that. The thing was that her success meant his failure, and his success meant her failure. It was an odd place to be, and if she cared to examine the situation even more closely, which she did not, she'd probably discover that in some ways she and Coulson were alike. Also, she'd probably see that she liked Coulson. Which was the reason why, halfway to the bar, she stopped, turned round and went back to her hospital. It was time to have a look at it. Food could wait, so could Coulson. Those were all peripheral distractions. Her hospital was not.

Not surprisingly, the front door was open. In fact, there was no lock on it. So she stepped inside and stood in the small lobby, just looking around, trying to picture it the way it would look in a few weeks, after she'd turned it into the place she wanted it to be. The lobby wasn't much larger than Coulson's waiting room and, to be honest, she was a little disappointed with that as it had looked larger in the photos he'd sent via the internet. But there was nothing she could do about that short of moving walls or building on, and there wasn't time for either of those right now. Maybe later. Right now she'd have to find a way for a lobby that seated ten, at best, to work.

Maybe move the reception desk out. It was small, but in the way. And the couple of small end tables…they didn't need to be there either. Yes, this could work, and suddenly she was feeling a little more optimistic.

Her optimism grew as she approached a set of swinging double doors separating what she guessed to be the treatment areas and patient rooms from the lobby. Stepping up to the doors, she stood on tiptoe, peeking in rather than going in. Even though she owned it now, it frightened her because it was only just dawning on her that this was her reality. Her *only* reality. Her future. And it seemed so… uncertain.

"It's going to need work," Adam said. "No one has occupied it as a medical facility for the better part of thirty years. A group of missionaries came in, built the hospital and several of the outbuildings for patients' families who had nowhere else to stay, and they operated the medical facilities here for about five years, then left."

"Why'd they leave?" she asked Adam.

"I've heard different stories. The area was too remote to be convenient…take the hint for your children's hospital, by the way. I also heard there weren't enough patients to keep it running…something else to consider in opening a children's hospital. Whatever the case, they evacuated during a hurricane and never came back…I'm not sure anybody knows the real reason. My guess is that they had good intentions that simply didn't work out the way they wanted. It happens. Could happen to you."

"You just don't give up, do you?" she asked, laughing.

"No, but maybe you will."

She shook her head, still smiling. "Don't think so, Coulson. It's a nice facility. A little smaller than I expected. But I like it."

"The bus only goes from village to village. We have service to the larger cities only three times a week, unless you have a car. Which makes a nice facility inconvenient for anyone not from the local area. Think about it, Red. You can't have a hospital if nobody comes."

"They'll come!" she exclaimed. "And being so remote is perfect." Her children didn't need to be bothered by the outside world. Here they'd find peace, as well as peace of mind. Two very essential ingredients in the healing process…something she knew immeasurably well.

"Well, your idea of perfect and mine aren't even close. Because if it were me trying to open up a hospital for any patients other than local, I'd be pretty concerned about the isolation."

"I'm not, though. And I don't look at this as isolated. I look at it as…separate. Set apart."

"I've got to hand it to you, Red. You're certainly the proverbial cockeyed optimist. Always seeing things the way you hope they'll be and not how they are."

"I guess maybe I am." She shoved through the double doors, fully expecting him to follow. Naturally, he did. "And just so you'll know, this hospital isn't going to fail and you're not going to get it back."

He chuckled. "That sure of yourself, are you?"

"Sure enough that I'm already having the bronze name plaque made."

"You know what they say about the best-laid schemes, don't you, Red?"

"The best-laid schemes o' mice an' men gang aft agley". The poet Robert Burns had been in a despondent place in his life when he'd written those words, and she'd been in that same kind of despondent place so many times, feeling her own plans go astray. But not this time. Her life was good now. She was looking forward, not backward. "What they say about *my* best-laid schemes is that they are so meticulously organized, they'll work out the way they're meant to." She smiled bravely, even though, deep down, she didn't feel that brave because she knew how it felt to want something very badly and not get it.

"I misspoke a moment ago. It's not cockeyed optimism." He arched playful eyebrows. "It's cocky confidence."

"And I'll take that as a compliment, because most of my life I've fought hard to achieve an honest level of confidence, and if you're seeing confidence of any level in me, then I've succeeded. Which means I'm even more prepared than I thought I was to make this hospital a success." Sure, she was being a little facetious, but mostly, she meant what she'd said. She'd lived most of her life without any appreciable level of confidence and to be told that her confidence was *showing* was good. Outstanding grades in medical school and excellent recommendations from the medical staff and instructors who'd supervised her notwithstanding, she'd always lived with such uncertainty. Sadly, uncertainty bred poor confidence. It couldn't have been avoided, because chronically sick children did tend to get tossed around emotionally. Her father had tried to help her through it. So had her childhood social worker, Mrs

Meecham, who'd long since turned into a fast family friend. And her psychologist, the one who'd worked with sick and dying children, had helped her, too. Maybe, though, that tag—sick and dying—more than anything else had held her back. Or possibly it was just the fact that for so much of her young life there had been no sure knowledge of anything. Nothing to look forward to.

Whatever the case, cocky confidence sounded amazing and Coulson couldn't have said anything better to her if he'd tried. "You sure do know how to turn a girl's head with your sweet talk, Coulson," she teased.

"Not to hear my ex-wife say it," he grumbled.

"Sounds ominous."

"Some days more than others."

She sensed that chapter in his life wasn't quite closed. She'd never really been in a married situation—not as a wife, not even as a daughter of a married couple. Her father was a lifelong confirmed bachelor, and her memories of her birth parents were so foggy they really didn't count for much of anything. "Well, I hope you're at a place where there are less ominous days than there are more." Vague words, but she really didn't have a right to pry.

"And I hope the same for you, except about the hospital. And in that, ominous for you means bright and sunny for me."

"How predictable," she quipped, taking her first glance down the corridor ahead of her. It was long, plain, with a few rooms on each side, and one large multi-bed ward at the far end. Nothing on the walls, nothing on the floors. Not even any bulbs in the light fixtures, she discovered, when she turned on the light. "It's going to work," she said, more to herself than to Coulson.

"Don't get your hopes up, Red. Making the necessary

changes and actually turning it into a functional hospital are two entirely different things."

"But the possibilities, Coulson… It's what my children need. Not the trappings they get in the hospitals they usually go to. It's about the possibilities."

"And that's supposed to mean?"

"So many things, but most of all hope. There's really so little hope inside four cold, white, clinical walls. I want more than that and my children deserve better than that. See, those beds in that first patient room…" She pointed to two beds with typical metal frames. Functional, sturdy, institutional. "There's no hope in those beds. They look like…typical hospital stock. But think about how very little it would take to turn them into something else, something that didn't remind the children of what they really were. It might just be as simple as a coat of red paint. Who knows?"

Coulson followed her into the large ward, which would bed the bulk of the hospital's patients. "And this…it's hideous. One big, open room. How can that be conducive to healing? Children need private space, a space where they can feel safe, not vulnerable the way they would with who knows how many other children sleeping almost on top of them." It would divide down into private cubicles, though, and no two would be the same because no two children were the same. It occurred to her that she might even be able to match a child to his room. "Don't you see it?" she asked in earnest.

"What I see is a pipe dream, and they rarely come true."

"Did you ever dream?"

"Once. Then I discovered it was more of a delusion. I loved her, thought I'd found the kind of dream of my heart you seem to think you've found in this hospital, thought she was something she wasn't."

"And?"

"In practical terms, she tried to suck me dry. Didn't want me coming back to Jamaica. Didn't want me working in a free medical practice. Wanted a big house with all the trappings. Wanted a life I didn't have to give her. What started out as a perfect dream dissolved into a nightmare."

"Leaving you bitter?"

"Leaving me wiser. Which is what I'm saying about this hospital, Red. You've got too many dreams riding on it, and it's going to break your heart. The things we want most in life always do."

"Spoken like a true cynic."

"Spoken from experience."

"But this hospital isn't going to break my heart. I won't let it."

"And you're not seeing the reality, just like I didn't see the reality in my wife. I saw what I wanted to. Fell in love with a vision that wasn't real."

"I'm sorry about your marriage, Coulson, but my vision is very real."

"Then time will tell, won't it?"

"I suppose it will." It seemed he'd lost a lot—his wife, his hospital, his dream. The best-laid schemes… Sad for him, but that was him, not her. Her best-laid schemes really were best-laid, whether or not she could convince him. And time would tell…tell Coulson that some dreams could come true.

Continuing down the hall, looking in room after room, nothing was appreciably different. It was a sturdy building, clean, well designed. Even more perfect for her plans than she'd expected. "How many patients will this place accommodate?"

"Thirty-two."

Just the right size. "Do you think it could be wired for ceiling fans or air-conditioning?"

"Sure. And you can lay down gold tiles, too, if you want them."

"Bitterness doesn't become you, Coulson." She did understand why he was bitter, though, and she truly didn't blame him because she would have been bitter, too, if this had turned out any other way than it had.

"It does when you disrupt my life." *And steal my dream.* But he was fighting hard to look on the bright side, even though being here now was throwing him back into the blues. He hadn't counted on this being so difficult, coming here and finally realizing once and for all, it was no longer his. It was hard to wrap his brain around that fact, hard to eulogize the dream gone dead. Still, his clinic would be better because of the sale of all this and, maybe, from that clinic, he could someday build a functioning hospital. Or, like he'd already warned her, buy this place back when her dream went bad. The truth was, though, he really didn't want that for her. It hurt, and she was so good-hearted in her intentions. But reality was reality and she wasn't seeing this situation for what it was. The only medical treatment this area needed was general care for the locals and since that wasn't her plan, her plan wasn't going to work. In that, he did feel bad.

Suddenly, he didn't like being back here. Not the way he used to like coming here. All he wanted to do was finish the tour and get out. "So, at the end of the hall, to the left, is the operating theater. It's small, doesn't have any equipment, but I think it can be turned into something respectable… if whatever kind of nontraditional hospital you're planning needs a surgery."

"We could. I'd have to make arrangements for a surgeon.

You wouldn't happen to be a surgeon by any chance, would you?"

"You're on your own when it comes to a surgeon. I'm a general practitioner. Able to do some basic minor surgical procedures. Definitely not about to attempt anything major." Another harsh reality for Erin. Getting a surgeon to come out here would be near to impossible. He'd tried, been turned down every polite way a man could be turned down. This area was too far out. The people here didn't pay, or paid very little. A nice basket of fresh fish was considered ample payment for services, and the surgeons he knew weren't into fresh fish. But Erin was going to go on believing she would wave a magic wand and produce a surgeon and that made him feel even worse.

The hell of it was, each time one of her dreams failed, it put him right back in the running for one of his to succeed. Yet she looked so...hopeful. It shimmered in her eyes. She was seeing this place as a fully running hospital, not the basic frame of something so impractical. For a moment he considered putting aside his plan and plunging head on into helping her with hers. But he couldn't. The people here needed more than some dreamy, half-thought-out idea that would never turn into a hospital for children. They needed a full-service medical facility, and he was going to give it to them. That's all there was to it. He refused to think any other way. "Are you ready for a nyamwich and bammys?"

"You go on," she said. "I want to stay here awhile longer. Think about what I'm going to do to get this place ready for the children. But thanks, anyway."

Damn, he hated her hopefulness. Because she truly believed in her purpose, and he didn't want to take that away from her inasmuch as he knew how it felt to have the hope ripped right out of him. It had been more than two years and that mess of his former life still returned to tweak him in some little, inexplicable way almost every day. Still, this situation with Erin Glover wasn't personal. She wanted to do something good here. So did he. Hence the impasse. However, the biggest difference was, his hospital was sensible, and very needed. Hers was a whim, a totally absurd expectation for the area based on factors she couldn't have possibly thought through. A romantic notion, that's what it was. And that's what he had to keep telling himself when he was inclined to get soft and give in. As getting soft toward Erin Glover seemed like an easy thing to do. Too easy.

Erin stood in the doorway of her hospital, watching Coulson walk over to Trinique's. Watching the little boy dart out of nowhere and shadow him, trying to match him step for step, trying to imitate the swagger she'd already come to know as exclusively Coulson. Cute boy. She'd seen him before, outside Trinique's, sitting on the step. Hadn't paid much attention as children scampered everywhere. That's one of the reason she loved it here. But this little boy…even from this far away, she could see that he adored Coulson. Did Coulson adore him back, though? She wanted to think that he was more than what she saw of his craggy exterior. And maybe he was. At least, the little boy seemed to think so. Kids usually had good instincts so maybe there was something more than met the eye with Adam Coulson.

Before going back inside her hospital, she watched Coulson and the boy a few more moments. Then suddenly all her apprehensions were alleviated in a simple gesture. Coulson reached over and tousled the boy's hair. It wasn't much, but it spoke volumes.

"Uncle Serek," Erin said, falling into the man's arms. He was a mountain of a man, large, fleshy, a grin so broad his ears wiggled when he smiled. At least, that's what she'd thought when she'd been a child. She had been almost college age when she'd learned that wiggling his ears was a trick meant only for her. "It's so good to see you."

"Erin," he said, hugging her the way a father would. "You get more beautiful every time I see you."

Serek Harrison was one of her father's oldest and dearest friends. A man who, over the years, had been wise in his advice on her own treatments. Her godfather, actually, not her uncle, even though that's what she'd always called him. Also an oncologist and head of the Port Wallace Public Hospital, he was semiretired now, and Erin believed with all her heart she owed part of her life to this dear man. "And the ocean breeze isn't taming my hair at all," she said, laughing. Prior to all her various times through chemotherapy, her hair had been more on the brownish side and definitely as straight as a board. Over the course of time, it had turned into a wild mane not completely out of control but close to it if she wasn't careful.

"It's beautiful hair," he said, in his smooth Jamaican lilt. "So, tell me, child. How is my old friend doing? I don't get very good feelings when I talk to him, and I haven't had time in the past few months to go to Chicago to visit him."

Pulling out of his arms, she sighed. "It's hard to tell. He doesn't talk about it. But he doesn't do much of anything nowadays either. He's totally quit his practice, as well as his position at the hospital. And while getting the children's hospital up and running has him interested, even that wasn't enough to motivate him to come here with me. And you know he's never passed up a chance to come home. But now he'd rather sit in his study, making phone calls, than be here." She drew in a shaky breath. "I'm worried about him,

Uncle Serek. I've never seen him like this and it scares me. It's like he doesn't have anything to live for any more."

"Well, Algernon is a stubborn man. Not prideful, but set in his own ways, and when he's fixed on doing something— like adopting a pretty little girl child no one wants him to have—you can't get him to change his mind."

"That's the problem. He's so set right now, and not set in a good way. He says he'll come down here when I'm ready to make the final move, and maybe he will, but I'm not even sure about that any more. Not sure about anything where my father is concerned."

"Walk with me, child. I have a patient to see in Emergency. One of our moonlighters, as you call them, is attending one of my Hodgkin patients for a non-related problem, and he wants me to come and have a look."

"You don't like moonlighters?" She was referring to physicians who worked various shifts at the hospital but were not regular employees. They were called moonlighters because more often than not they worked the dreaded night shift, the shift regulars liked to avoid when possible.

"We love our moonlighters. Have a very good one I'm afraid we're going to lose shortly. Or so I've just been informed. Of course, if you're moving to the island permanently..." He grinned. "I can be persuasive, Erin. I'll give you my time for your kiddies like I've already promised, and maybe you can give me a little of your time for my emergency department. Does that seem like a fair exchange?"

"If you want to take a chance, because I haven't worked in Emergency since I was in medical school." Of course, she hadn't worked in obstetrics since med school either, and that's what Coulson had her doing.

"It's like riding a bicycle. Once you learn how to do it,

you never forget." He sobered. "Did you ever get to ride a bicycle when you were a child?"

"By the time I was well enough to play outside, I was old enough to drive a car. So, no, I never got around to the bicycle."

"Then someone will just have to teach you. To live on the island, you must have a bicycle."

"Do you?"

"Mercy, no! I have a very nice automobile, and a wife who delights in driving me because she believes I drive too fast. But maybe you and I will have time to learn to ride a bicycle together."

"Bicycle paths…" she whispered absently.

"Excuse me?"

"Bicycle paths. Around the hospital. My children will need bicycles because I think some of them will be able to ride. Maybe not the two-wheelers, but I'm sure some will be able to handle the three-wheelers. So we'll need riding paths."

"My donation, then. Bicycles and a bicycle path. Along with someone to teach you to ride."

"All that, plus your time?" What an amazing man. She loved him nearly as much as she did her father.

"It's worthy, and it will give me something to do in my retirement. Besides, if I learn how to ride, and you have those bicycle paths laid in, that will give me more excuses to come visit my old friend and his lovely daughter." He shoved through the open doors to the emergency department then held them open for Erin. "And I won't let Algernon go to waste, Erin. You have my word on that. I love that man like he's my own brother, and I'm glad he's coming home, where he can be around his friends. He'll find himself here." He gave her another huge hug. "We'll make sure of that."

"You don't know how that makes me feel, hearing you say it," she sniffled.

He chuckled. "And you don't know how it makes me feel knowing that you'll be here, moonlighting, every once in a while. Or spending time with Alvinnia and me, when you're able. You're a daughter to her, you know. Now, put on a white coat and come and see this patient with me. And the doctor you'll be meeting is quite interesting, too. A head-strong fellow, but good." He grinned his infamous grin. "Handsome, too, and, if I'm not mistaken, single. Don't know him well. Wasn't the one to hire him, but I've heard good reports of his skills. And did I mention handsome? So maybe you can get to know him in due course?"

"You sound just like my father," she said, swatting playfully at his arm. "He'd turn himself into a doting old matchmaker if I ever gave him the least little bit of encouragement."

"Because your father is worried he won't get grandchildren. And I'm worried I won't get grand-godchildren. We're turning into old men, child. And old men need children around them to keep them young. You wouldn't deprive us of that, would you?"

"I'll have plenty of children for you at the hospital. And right now I'm really just interested in getting it going. No entanglements."

"Even if they're handsome?"

"*Especially* if they're handsome." As they strolled through the tiny emergency department, Erin was impressed by what she saw. Emergency was full to overflowing, but people were patiently awaiting their turns to be seen. "And I especially don't want an entanglement if it comes in the form of a…" Pushing through the curtain in cubicle number three, where Serek's patient waited, Erin stopped dead in her tracks. "In the form of *him!*"

Adam turned round, didn't smile at her, but definitely looked surprised to see her. "Are you following me?" he asked.

Serek looked first at Adam then at Erin as a sly grin spread across his face. "So you two know each other?"

"It's his hospital I bought," she explained.

"You own a hospital, Adam?" Serek asked. "You never told me that."

"Used to own one. Not operational. Sold it to…" He nodded toward Erin.

"It's what I bought for the children's hospital. And he thinks I won't be able to make it work."

"Well, I had no idea that's where you lived, Adam. But it's certainly a small world, isn't it, with you working here and Erin buying your hospital? You two have quite a connection."

"Then *you two* know each other?" Adam asked.

"I'm trying to convince Erin to come and moonlight for me." Serek grinned. "And since you two seem to be living in the same area, maybe you could ride in together. It's a long drive, and you can keep each other company. And, Erin, child. Alvinnia's going to be so excited by all this."

"Alvinnia?" Coulson questioned, clearly confused.

"My wife," Serek replied.

"My godmother," Erin added. "And Serek is my godfather, by the way." She latched onto the older man's arm. "He's also one of the volunteer doctors who'll be coming to my hospital. Along with Aunt Alvinnia…she's a surgeon."

"Well, I'll be damned. You're actually getting a surgeon?" Coulson looked first at Serek then at Erin and it wasn't her imagination that made her think she heard a loud, discouraging sigh escape his lips. She did, and she saw the look of disappointment on his face. Rather than the satisfaction she'd expected to feel, she actually felt sad for him. Another best-laid scheme *gang agley*. He couldn't even hide the disappointment. Of course he'd thought she would fail and go away. Of course he'd thought he would swoop in then and pick up the pieces and be all the better for her defeat. Yet there wasn't great triumph in this victory and she did feel bad for him.

Not bad enough to give up her hospital, though. "Yep, I'm getting a surgeon." Which meant Erin was one step closer to her dream while Coulson was one step further from his. What concerned her about this situation, however, was that she cared that he was a step further away. She wasn't sure why she cared, but she did. And it was unsettling.

CHAPTER FOUR

THE one thing that was for certain with a good boat—the hull didn't give way. That's what his grandfather had said the day he'd decided to sink the boat and let it spend its eternity on the ocean floor, building up a coral reef and habitat for little sea creatures. The *Stella*, as his grandfather had named it, had almost given way with a hole so large in its hull that the expert boat repair shops in Portland had all turned it down. Quite simply, it would have been less expensive to buy a new boat. And Cornelius Coulson, not being a man who cared to wander too far from home to look for any more marine repair shops, had taken that as a sign. He'd run aground on an outcropping of rocks one time and survived, and he wasn't going to tempt fate by repairing the boat and risking another rock outcropping. Better to allow nature to reclaim the wooden 1951 Lyman Islander than let it claim him or anybody he'd loved, his grandfather always said.

But Adam had begged to keep the boat. For a playhouse. Or they could turn it into a pretend fort or even a make-believe pirate ship. All imaginative plans for a ten-year-old. Luckily, Grandpa Coulson had seen merit in turning *Stella*, named after his wife, into a toy. And that's how Adam Coulson had become the only kid in his school who owned his own boat. Albeit one that wasn't sea-, river-, or pond-worthy.

Twenty-six years later, he still owned the boat. It was his legacy from an extraordinary man and pretty much the only thing his wife hadn't wanted to snatch away from him in the divorce. *Stella* kept him grounded as a man, and testified to the fact that nothing was futile if you wanted it badly enough. She was nearly sea-worthy again. It had taken him the better part of the past ten years to bring her back to this point, an hour here, a few minutes there. And while he didn't fancy himself as a master ship repairman, he'd taken a fair amount of pride in the project. Wished his grandfather could have seen the transformation. Oh, there were still some minor things to do…a bit more varnish, some work to unwarp the warped deck, a new wheel… nothing insurmountable. Which was why, when he took to sanding the deck, like he was doing today, he felt his spirits lifting. *Stella* was a symbol of what he could do. So was the white building sitting off in the distance. The hospital. The courts had seen fit to let him keep a modest inheritance from his grandfather, along with *Stella*, and he'd celebrated that small victory by buying the hospital with that inheritance. Except that was half-gone now. But maybe that was good. He was trying hard to think so, anyway.

"It's all good," he muttered, crawling forward on his hands and knees to the plastic cooler with the bottle of water. He grabbed the water and two cups, poured and handed one cup across to his companion who sat opposite him on the deck, cross-legged. "It has to be all good, Tadeo," he said to the bright-eyed boy who came so often to the beach to help him with the boat that working on the boat without Tadeo didn't seem right. "Because if it's not, then what's the point?"

"All good," Tadeo agreed, smiling.

"So, what kind of sandpaper do we need to use over in that corner of the deck?" He pointed to the right stern. Another source of pride these days—Tadeo. He'd gone from withdrawn to involved. His skills at boat refurbishing weren't bad either, for a kid his age.

"Fine grit. To finish it. Then extra-fine, before we do the varnish."

Yes, Tadeo had come a long way these past few months, and the change was satisfying to Adam. But it also pointed out something painfully obvious…how absolutely, totally alone he was in the world. He looked at Davion as a protégé, and Tadeo as a protégé as well. He was doing things with them he'd have loved doing with his own son…except for the obvious. He didn't have a son. But what could he expect? He couldn't hang on to a relationship that might give him a son or daughter and, more than that, he didn't particularly live a lifestyle that would be attractive to a woman. No stability, no woman, no children. There was definitely a pattern there. Or maybe it was a habit. Didn't matter, though. Alone was alone, any way you stated it.

His mind wandered to Erin. She had such…stability. It suited her. Became her. And he had…well, an old boat, a transient medical practice, and several odd jobs. Nothing someone stable would want. Not that he would even consider *having* anything with Erin. Or maybe it was the other way around. She wouldn't consider having anything to do with him. Didn't matter. It was what it was, and he was good with that. "The varnish is a way off," he explained to Tadeo. "Especially when we're doing all the work the old-fashioned way…by hand." No sander, no tools. Just what his grandfather called elbow grease. And it was a good thing to teach Tadeo, like it had been a good thing taught by his grandfather. *Life moves too fast, Adam. Sometimes it's nice to slow down and enjoy the process. There's a good view, and a good lesson in the process if you look for it.* How many times had he heard those words? Well, this was the process and the view was good, especially when he watched Tadeo taking it all in.

"But you'll let me help?" Tadeo asked.

"Couldn't do it without you. And you remember what I promised?"

"That I'll be the first one to steer the boat once you get it away from the dock."

He gave Tadeo a thumbs-up. "The very first one." It wasn't much for all the hours Tadeo had put in, but Tadeo clung to that promise like *he'd* clung to the very same promise of steering the boat when his grandfather had made it to him.

"Are you busy?" Erin called from the bow.

Adam rose, waved her aboard. "Use the ladder, and watch your step. It could shift in the sand." Naturally, he stood to help her, but by the time he'd got to the side to extend a hand, she'd already scrambled over the rail.

"That's the ma'am doc," Tadeo said, shrinking back against the side.

"He's shy with strangers," Adam explained to Erin.

Erin kept a respectful distance from the boy. "My name's Erin," she said to him. "And I used to be shy, too."

His eyes widened, but he said nothing.

"But if you'd like to tell me your name, I'd certainly like to know."

Tadeo thought about it for a moment, the full weight of a serious decision scrunching up his face. Then, gravely, he nodded. "Good afternoon, ma'am. I'm Tadeo, ma'am. Tadeo Alejandro Reyes."

"Good afternoon, Tadeo Alejandro Reyes. It's nice to meet you," she said, trying as hard as she could to be serious when all she really wanted to do was break out in a grin, the boy was so cute. But his serious demeanor set her tone, and she stayed serious as well. "I'll be living here all the time, so maybe we'll see each other again."

His answer was to pick up a piece of sandpaper and go back to work on the decking.

"Cute little boy," Erin whispered to Adam.

"Good helper, too. Shows some definite skill in woodworking. So, what brings you to my side of the property line? Come to admire my boat?"

"Your boat?"

"The only thing I have left after both you and my ex-wife got through with me."

"Am I detecting some bitterness about women in general, Coulson?"

"Never bitter when I'm on my boat," he said, stroking the smooth wooden deck rail like it was the smooth flesh of a woman. "She's the one woman who won't ever let me down."

"Looks like it's been around for a while."

"She. *She's* been around for a while. Longer than any other female in my life, come to think of it."

"Well, never let it be said that I came between a man and his boat. So…" he held out a box to him "…take this, then I'll leave you to get back to whatever it is you're doing with your boat."

"Sanding," Tadeo said. "Then we're going to start varnishing."

"He's anxious to move on to the next phase of restoration," Adam commented, taking the box. "Couldn't get this boat back into shape without him. So…if I open this, will something jump out and bite me?"

"Just open it, Coulson. I'm trying to make a nice gesture here, and you're ruining it."

"Nice gestures involve giving me back my hospital, but since my hospital won't fit into the box…" He opened the lid. Studied the stethoscope for a moment, then pulled it out and put it around his neck. "Tadeo," he said. "Come over here. I want to try something out."

The boy obliged, taking care not to walk too close to Erin. When she noticed, she stepped back to give him freer passage to Adam. "What is it?" he asked.

"Haven't you ever been examined by a doctor?" Adam asked, frowning.

Tadeo shook his head. "Pabla says we don't need doctors. Sometimes Trinique looks at me, but never a doctor."

"Pabla's his guardian," he explained to Erin. Then, to Tadeo, "Well, we're about to fix that. This is called a stethoscope, and when I put it on your chest, I'll be able to hear your heart beating." He smiled up at Erin. "Unless ma'am Doc would rather I examine her first."

"Ma'am Doc is just fine without an examination," Erin said, as little skittery goosebumps trotted their way up her arms. Something about seeing Coulson with pants cut well above his knees and an unbuttoned cotton shirt revealing a rather nicely bronzed, hairless chest was attracting attention from her she hadn't known she had for him. He was all lean, in amazing proportions, and thinking about all that virility laying a hand to her chest, albeit a hand holding a stethoscope, shook her all the way down to her toes. "But thank you for asking," she said, hoping her voice didn't sound as unsteady as she suddenly felt.

"And thank you for the stethoscope," he replied, holding up the bell in salute. "I do appreciate this, Red, and just for you being so kind, I promise not to bother you about the hospital for the next twenty-four hours."

"A promise made before that you haven't kept yet."

"Well, this time I'll keep it."

She smiled. "I'll believe that when I *don't* hear it."

"You wound me, Red. When I make a promise, I always intend to keep it." He arched playful eyebrows at her. "You'll just have to keep reminding me."

Which would put them in closer proximity than she wanted. "Like I said before, Coulson. I'll believe it when I *don't* hear it." She rubbed her arms, trying to fight back the multiplying goosebumps, cursing inwardly that he always did that to her.

He winked at Tadeo, who smiled back at him. "One of the lessons you're going to have to learn about women, Tadeo, is that no matter how hard you try to convince them, it's never hard enough. They make you work for it."

"Why?" he asked, innocently.

"Yes, Coulson. I'd like to hear why."

"That's the nature of a woman," he said, trying to keep a straight face.

"Or is it the nature of a woman who's trying to stand her ground against the nature of a man?"

Tadeo, clearly bored with the repartee between the two, picked up the bell of the stethoscope and laid it to his belly. Adam quickly adjusted it, smiling at Erin. "I think he's trying to tell us something."

"Out of the mouths of babes..." The air between them was practically sparking and it totally confounded her how an innocent conversation over nothing could turn into something else. But it had. One wink, one arch of the eyebrow and she had been seduced.

"Babes who have other things on their minds," he said, inserting the earpieces. "Now, Tadeo, this isn't going to hurt at all. All I'm going to do is listen. Nothing's going to poke you." Bell to the chest, he started to listen. Looked up at Erin... "Nice," he murmured. "Excellent resonance." He moved the bell a couple of times, nodding, listening.

Amazing, Erin thought, how something taken so for granted in the medical world was so important. She'd never thought about a stethoscope. There'd always been one around. Her father's. Then hers. And Adam was acting like a child on Christmas morning over a simple thing.

"Can I hear?" Tadeo asked, shyly.

"Just a minute," he said absently. Then moved the bell to another location. "I think ma'am Doc should get to listen next, since she's the one who gave me the stethoscope."

Normally, she didn't share earpieces. Always used her own stethoscope or swabbed the one she was going to use if it wasn't hers, but something odd in Adam's expression caused her to break her own rule. So, without a word, she bent down, took the stethoscope from him and had a listen. "When you were born," she asked casually, "was it at home, or in a hospital?"

Tadeo shrugged.

Erin glanced up at Adam, whose face had drained of most of its color. Then she mouthed the word "murmur."

He nodded. "Tadeo, how about I let you listen to your heart a little later? I need to go over to the clinic for a while, see if I have any patients, check some supplies…"

"OK," Tadeo agreed. "But can I stay here on the boat?"

"'Fraid not, sport. You know what I've told you about not getting up on the boat when I'm not here with you. That's the rule you can't break. But here's what we're going to do. Come to the clinic later on, and I'll let you listen to your heart, and to mine. OK?" He nodded sideways at Erin. "And maybe she can show you some other medical tests she likes to do. Sound good to you?"

Obviously not as good as working on the boat, but Tadeo agreed, then scampered down over the side and ran off through a thicket of palms toward his house. Adam watched him for a minute then finally turned to face Erin. "I'd say it's at least a three, maybe a four. And he was resting." Heart murmurs were graded on a system of one through six, with one being the weakest, six being the strongest. "Damn it to hell, I work with the kid almost every day. Have meals with him, play with him. How could I have not known?"

"Because he's your friend, not your patient. And his guardian hasn't taken him to see a doctor. He probably wasn't born in a hospital, so he didn't get diagnosed then. So don't beat yourself up about this, Coulson. It's not like you can even hear a heart murmur when you're not listening to his chest."

He slammed his fist on the deck rail. "Son of a... I haven't seen symptoms, Red. Not a damn one."

"And he may not have symptoms. You know as well as I do that most childhood heart murmurs are innocent. They don't cause problems, and kids outgrow them. I've treated dozens of kids with innocent heart murmurs, none of them ever had any consequences and, as a matter of fact, none of them have ever shown any outward symptoms."

"But what if it's not innocent?"

"That's a huge leap at this point. Right now I'd suggest we get him diagnosed properly. Take him into the hospital at Port Wallace, get a chest X-ray, some blood work done, an EKG, maybe an echocardiogram, depending on the results of everything else." She knew Adam felt horrible but a heart murmur often signified nothing. It was a noise that the blood made as it flowed through the heart. When she described the condition to parents, she likened it to the noise water made when it flowed through a hose, telling them that these noises were easily heard in children because their hearts were very close to their chest walls. Then she'd reassure them that heart murmurs were common and that, in fact, age and physical growth usually took care of them. Especially when it was what was commonly called an *innocent* or *functional* heart murmur.

Naturally, some murmurs indicated more serious problems, but she never made that leap without tests. Adam, however, was already making that leap. She could see it in his face. "Why don't you go talk to his guardian, get her permission for more testing, make sure she knows she's welcome to come along with us, then we'll both take Tadeo to the public hospital?"

"What if it's not innocent?" he asked, turning his back to her and standing, wide-stanced, where he could look out over the ocean. His hand visored his eyes from the sun, his normally-squared shoulders slumped. "What if he's got a stenosis, a leak, or, God forbid, a hole? What then?"

"We'll fix it."

"It's not that easy out here, Red. I know you've got all kinds of good, probably impossible, intentions with your children's hospital, but those rose-colored glasses don't work out here in the middle of nowhere."

"I know Jamaica, Coulson."

He spun to face her. "Because you were a tourist here a few times, and you fell in love with the conch fritters and the gauze skirts they sell in the tourist shops? Is that how you know Jamaica?"

"I know it through my father."

"That's right. He was the one who brought you on vacation here, wasn't he? Probably to see your affluent godfather?"

She knew he was angry. And she wasn't going to provoke him because he felt bad enough as it was. But his characterization of her wasn't fair. Not at all. "My father was born in Jamaica, in a small town called Alligator Pond. Ever hear of it?"

She could tell by his face that he had. "My grandmother owned a fishing business there. She and my grandfather started with nothing and made a success of it. And that's what my father comes from, not the tourist side of the island. So when you say I don't know the island, you're right in some ways. I've never lived here. But I know it through my father, and I know the difficulties ahead for Tadeo if his heart murmur turns out to be serious. I also know there's hope here for him."

"Who are you, Red? Who are you, really?"

"By parentage, I am Jamaican. The daughter of a Jamaican. The daughter of Algernon Glover."

That one caught him by surprise. "Dr Algernon Glover?"

Erin nodded. "Dr Algernon Glover."

"Aren't you just full of surprises? Goddaughter of Serek Harrison…daughter of the legendary Algernon Glover."

"And what's that supposed to mean?" she asked. She was used to the stares, to the comments people made behind her back. Her father had gone to hell and back because it hadn't been seemly to adopt her. Single black man adopting a sickly white girl…the odds had been stacked against them. But none of it mattered because her father hadn't given up on her then, and because of that she was here now, fighting with Adam Coulson.

"What it's supposed to mean is that things are different now. Before, when I was fighting Erin Glover for that thing I said I wouldn't talk about, I was fighting a naive doctor with an impractical dream. Then you threw Serek Harrison and his wife into the mix and I'll admit that's when I started to worry that my odds were insurmountable. Because, Red, I thought that, at some point, you'd give up and I'd buy that unspeakable thing back. I've made no secret of that. But now that I'm fighting the daughter of Algernon Glover…"

"Why does it have to be a fight? I thought we were past that."

"You're past it. I'm not."

"Can we get over that hump, Coulson? Or will it always pop out, always come back to jab me? Because I don't want it to be this way. Because we're neighbors now. I'm staying and you're not going. And we're going to have medical interests in common. But it's not up to me to change anything between us because I'm not the one having the problem."

"Look, Red, I'm sorry. Giving it up doesn't come easy for me, as you're seeing. Ask my ex-wife. I was holding on tenaciously even after the ink had dried on the divorce document, still fighting to keep a little piece of that dream even when I knew it was dead."

"Because you loved her that much?"

He shook his head. "Because I'm that stubborn. I don't like to give up. It's my nature. I hate quitting on anything."

She laughed. "So you would have held on to a bad marriage because you were stubborn?"

"Actually, I would have held on to some of the marital assets. But let's just say that split wasn't exactly equitable."

"You mean she took you?"

He cringed. "Lock, stock and barrel. But, in her defense, I suppose she was entitled. I was using marital assets to fund some of my medical ventures here. Didn't ask her, just did it. I assumed she'd feel the same way about it as I did, but I was wrong. And she accused me of leaving her out of important decisions, which I did. Good intentions, bad outcome. But the breakdown was already in the works. She was corporate medicine and I was…all this, and pretty damned stubborn on top of it." He gestured to the area around him. "No excuses, but this was me, heart and soul, from the first time I set foot on the island and saw that I could truly make a difference here. Anyway, I don't think we knew that about each other when we got married, and over time, when the honeymoon was over and our real desires came out, I think I just found it easier to skip the communication since we really didn't agree on much of anything. That's the simplified version of a very complicated situation but, whatever the case, what had started so well ended badly and I'll admit I get a good bit of the blame for the failure."

"Like you're going to take a good bit of the blame for being so stubborn with me?"

"You don't give up, do you, Red?" he asked, laughing.

"Well, I've been accused of being stubborn, too. I'll admit it." She arched playful eyebrows. "But not too emphatically. In the meantime, I'd suggest we take our stubborn selves over to Tadeo's guardian and have a talk with her about his condition. I'll feel better when we can have him properly diagnosed."

"You don't have to be involved in this."

She shrugged. "I already am. Something about a child in need gets me every time."

But things didn't go as well with Pabla Reyes as they'd hoped for. "No doctors," she said, folding vehement arms across her chest. "Don't believe in them, don't want them, don't have the money to pay for them. *Don't like them interfering in something that's none of their business.* Since Tadeo has done fine all this time, with this so-called murmur, I'm not changing things now."

Erin looked at Adam, not sure what to do. They'd been there ten minutes already, and Miss Reyes didn't seem the least bit concerned about what they'd told her. Erin had stated her case, done everything short of begging on her hands and knees, and every word was falling on deaf and extremely hostile ears. Pabla Reyes reminded Erin of her own parents. They hadn't wanted to pay for her medical care, hadn't wanted to deal with a sick child, which had turned into refusing to get her medical help. As hard as it was to believe, it happened. The social services systems were full of sick kids who'd been abandoned by parents who couldn't, or wouldn't, cope. From what she'd been told about her own parents years later, they weren't poor. More likely, they hadn't wanted the inconvenience. So one day they'd simply dropped her off at a nursing home. Literally checked her in, said they'd be back to see her the next day, and never returned. She'd waited...days, weeks, months, and nothing.

It hadn't been a bad facility, all things considered. But it hadn't been a facility meant for a child who had been so sick, so scared... She knew that anguish, still felt it. Felt a little of it now, for Tadeo, because if his condition turned out to be more than innocent... "Look, if you change your mind about this, come and tell us. OK? The only thing we want to do here is help Tadeo."

"But you said it might be nothing," Pabla Reyes argued. "Which means you don't know, and I'm not doing anything about something you don't know."

"And she also said it might be *something*," Adam argued back.

"Would if make any difference to you if I offered to pay for everything?" Erin asked.

"You think I don't take good care of the boy?"

Now Erin was fighting to keep her opinion to herself because she didn't know what kind of a caregiver Pabla Reyes was, but from where she was standing at this moment Miss Reyes wasn't looking all that good. "What I think is that the tests are a simple thing, and I'd hoped you'd be anxious to know the results."

"Trinique never said anything about this murmur," the woman contended.

"Trinique owns a bar. She's not a nurse or a doctor."

Pabla pointed an accusatory finger at Adam. "And that one works at the bar, too. And calls himself a doctor but he can't even pour a decent rum."

Adam took hold of Erin's arm with the purpose of tugging her toward the door. She knew that. Which was why she shrugged away from him. Suddenly this argument with Pabla was becoming personal. It reminded her of all the fights she'd overheard her parents have. And the fights her social worker, Mrs Meecham, had had with them as well. Bad days leading up to the day they'd abandoned her. Days she didn't want to remember, but Pabla's refusal was dredging up the old memories, which was bringing out the fight in her. "He's a very good doctor…a doctor who cares a great deal for Tadeo."

Pabla turned her attention to Adam. "He's not yours to be concerned with, Doctor, and I want you to stay away from him. If you don't, I'll call the authorities."

"Call them," Adam snapped. "And while you're at it, tell them you're the one who's refusing Tadeo medical care. Tell them you're the child's guardian who doesn't give a—"

This time Erin was the one who tried getting the two of them out of there. Grabbing Adam's arm, she tugged, met with resistance, and tugged harder. Hard enough to catch his attention and, once that was caught, she nodded toward the door. Put on the sternest face she had, and hoped it was enough. Because she was angry, Adam was angrier and who in the world knew what Pabla Reyes was other than downright wrong?

"Think about it, Miss Reyes. Tadeo needs the tests, and we'll see to all the arrangements." Those were her last words, the end of her argument, and she felt totally defeated as she walked out the door. Walking slowly, hoping Pabla Reyes would have a change of heart before she and Adam were completely away from there. But that didn't turn out to be the case. In fact, by the time she'd reached the front door, with Adam following close behind, Pabla Reyes had left the room.

"Poor kid," Adam muttered as they wandered along the sandy path, winding in and out of the palm trees. "I've always suspected it was bad for him here. Didn't know how much. But with a guardian like that…"

"Do you think she'll change her mind?" Erin asked.

"Who knows? I think it's pretty clear she doesn't want to be bothered, which would be fine if Tadeo didn't have a heart murmur. But how the hell could anyone refuse him the tests when we've done everything but offered to have the equipment brought here?"

"Maybe she's scared. A lot of people avoid the inevitable by not admitting it."

"If it's their own condition, I get that. I avoided the inevitable in my marriage for along time by not admitting what was going on around me. But this is an adult who has custody of a child with a medical condition, and it doesn't matter how scared *she* is. It's not about her."

"Well, all I can say is that it certainly didn't work out the way I thought it would." She was so discouraged her steps felt weighted in the sand. "And you're right. It's hard to believe…" She was going to say that it was hard to believe that someone could have so little concern for a child's health and welfare but, actually, she *could* believe that because it had been a fact of her own life for most of it. "So, is there anything else we can do?"

"Short of abducting Tadeo and taking him to the hospital? No, there's not."

"Even though she could be compromising Tadeo's health?"

Adam exhaled an annoyed sigh, stopped on the trail, leaned up against an old, bent-over palm tree. "I suppose we could have lied to her, said it was serious, and not even mentioned the strong possibility that it's innocent."

Erin turned round to face him. Admired the rugged stance of him. Adam Coulson was as casual a man as she'd ever met, but he wore his masculinity right out there to be seen by anyone who cared to look. And while she didn't like admitting it, she cared to look. In her world the men were constrained. Their casual was tan slacks and yellow polo shirts. They didn't go around with their chests exposed the way Adam did. Admittedly, she was finding that she had a preference for bare chests, and just for a moment she pictured his bronzed, bare chest under an open, white, perfectly starched lab coat. With his brand-new stethoscope hanging down the middle of his chest, of course. It was an image she forced herself to blink away before her knees wobbled out from underneath her. "Wouldn't you have some kind of an ethical problem doing that?" she asked, her voice just a tad higher than usual.

"Huge ethical problem, because I don't lie. Won't lie. But it makes me wonder what I'd have done, or said, if I'd known for sure that his heart murmur was serious. I don't want to be put in a position that I'd ever have to violate any kind of medical ethic, but what about the child who clearly doesn't have the kind of advocacy he or she needs? Would I go against my ethics to take care of that child?" He stared directly at her, the deep concern showing in his eyes. "You're a pediatrician, Red. Would you do what you had to in order to protect a child, even if it did, in some way, go against what we've learned is ethical in the practice of medicine?"

"To save a child?" She didn't even have to think. Her adoptive father had gone against convention to save her. Because of him, in her life the children always came first. That's why she was here, in Jamaica. "I'd do what I had to do. My father has always believed that our duty to our fellow man is a privilege and an honor, but he's always said that privilege and honor don't come without sacrifices. To save a child, I would...*will*...make the sacrifices I have to." She thanked God every day of her life that her father had done what he had to do to save her.

"Wise man," Adam said, almost reverently.

"He is." And there was still need for Algernon Glover's wisdom, even if he didn't believe it to be so.

"And I'll bet he's patient, too. Not like me, because I'm so damned angry that someone could be so irresponsible I want to kick something." He eyed the palm tree, opted not to. "It doesn't make sense to me."

"It happens, though," Erin said. "Parents, guardians... adults in general don't always act in the best interests of their children. But for Tadeo, we've got to find a way around it. This Trinique...would she have some influence with Miss Reyes?"

"Trinique has her own influence with the people in her little corner of the world. But would she convince Pabla that Tadeo needs some medical tests? Hell, I don't know. And it's an irrelevant point anyway, because I don't think she's coming back for a while. Davion said his aunt has taken a turn for the worse and Trinique's going to stay there for as long as she has to. Meaning..." He shrugged. "I don't even know what that means except that, besides the two of us, there's no one here to fight for Tadeo."

"You really care for him, don't you?"

"He's a good kid. Reminds me of myself when I was his age. Always underfoot, always inquisitive. I have great parents, but they were away a lot when I was a kid. My dad traveled on business, my mom was a surgeon and on call most of the time. So my grandfather stepped in. He was the one who answered the questions, taught me how to get along in the world. In fact, when I think back on my childhood, it's my grandfather who comes to mind first, because he was my greatest influence. Like I said, my parents were great, but to me they were always off in the background somewhere. So it was my grandfather's solid influence I needed, he was my best friend. And I don't think Tadeo has that anywhere, from anyone. Definitely not from Pabla."

"He has that from you, Coulson. And you may have to fight Pabla to maintain that place in his life. So, are you willing to do that for him?"

Adam nodded. "Whatever it takes, because it's like he's out there in the world, trying to figure it out on his own. I know Pabla lets him wander around all hours of the day and night. Probably doesn't have any idea where he is, and probably doesn't even care. Half the time, when I'm tending bar at Trinique's, Tadeo will be waiting outside on the step for me when I get off work, or he'll be sleeping in the hammock I have strung up at my cottage."

Then it was a good thing he had Coulson because somehow, some way, she trusted with all her heart that Coulson would come through for the boy no matter what else happened. It made her feel better believing in that. "I think the only thing we can do at this point is watch him. If we see symptoms of *anything* happening, then we try talking to Pabla again. Or contact the authorities if she won't cooperate."

"Not we, Red. Like I said before, you're not involved in this. And dealing with Pabla could get ugly."

That stung. Especially since she was already so emotionally involved. "But I am involved, Coulson. You drew me in and what do you expect me to do? Just stand back and watch a bad situation get worse? Watch it and not do anything to fix it? Because that's not me."

"I know it's not you. And this isn't anything personal. But I'm a solo act here, Red, and I want to keep it that way."

"Even after you were the one who wanted me to work in your clinic, and even go with you to talk to Pabla?"

"Even after all that. And I appreciate it. But we're not attached at the hip. We have our separate ways to go. And like I said, Pabla has a reputation for getting...ugly."

"I don't need someone protecting me, Coulson, if that's what you're trying to do. I can take care of myself with Pabla Reyes. Probably as well as I can set up a hospital and run it. So don't worry about me, because I'm not about to attach myself to anybody's hip. Least of all yours!" Still, she did see his side of it, and he was right. As much as she wanted to be involved with Tadeo, Coulson was better suited to handle the situation. So maybe it was time she put up her own dividing line because it was so easy to get drawn over to his side. Otherwise she'd never finish what she'd come here to start. Did Coulson see that in her? Did he see how easily she got emotionally involved? Or was him pushing her back to her own work a sign of him softening toward the hospital? She certainly hoped so. "Oh, and just so you know, the architects will be here day after tomorrow and, with any luck, we'll be starting renovations within the next couple of weeks. So you won't have to worry about me getting too close to your hip again as I'll be pretty busy with my own concerns. The first one being the transformation of the hospital building."

He flinched visibly. "Meaning?"

"Meaning blue, for starters. Kids deserve blue, not white."

"You're not serious...blue?"

"Very serious, and very blue. Studies show that it's the favorite color among children, and while I haven't decided the exact shade of blue I want to use, I thinking something bright, happy. And each of the outbuildings...red, purple, green, orange, yellow... I'm very serious about that, too! Shortly your plain old white is going to turn into a rainbow." Spinning, she strolled off in the direction of her medical compound, feeling a little optimistic that Coulson's sentiment toward the hospital really was changing for the better. Still, seeing his reaction to the colors she'd chosen did sting a little as she didn't want her decisions to slap him, but that's exactly what she'd done, and she didn't feel good about it. In the end, no matter what she did, he was always going to look at her as the person who had stolen his dream. There might be easy moments between them from time to time, maybe even times when they worked together again. But overall they were at such great odds she couldn't see much of a truce in the offing. He kept saying it wasn't personal. But it was. This situation with Adam Coulson was very personal.

CHAPTER FIVE

THREE days, three nights and they'd avoided each other, not so much by design but by happenstance. Which was hard to do, considering how they lived on the same plot of land, separated by only a few palm trees and some sand. But she was keeping to her side of the imaginary line and he to his. He'd taken down the ropes, even though that line between them was still implied. At least, it was to him, and she was doing a good job of observing it, too. Of course, she had no reason to come over to his side, and while he might have been interested in watching the progress to her hospital, he just couldn't look because…blue! Selling the hospital was one thing, but painting it blue… He cringed thinking about it. The thing was, he didn't hate blue. It was the color of the ocean, of the sky…nice color. But on a hospital?

Actually, it was more the symbolism of painting the hospital blue than it was the color, but it just struck him as wrong. Or maybe wrong because he'd always seen the hospital as white, couldn't imagine it being anything other than what it was, couldn't see it being any color other than what it was. OK, so maybe he was being stubborn about this. But he didn't have to like blue.

Although being white, the way it was now, it was also doomed to being empty. Sure, he was overreacting to the changes. Especially as she was doing a noble thing, turning an empty building into something good and useful. Misguided but noble, and deep down he was cheering her on. But she was getting to him. Making him think about her. Making him wish for things he knew he couldn't or shouldn't have. The honest truth was, Erin Glover fascinated him and he'd caught himself watching her from afar too many times now. Not a good sign. He'd pushed her away all those days ago for his own good, not hers. She distracted him and he caught himself wanting to be distracted. Caught himself not minding being attached at the hip. And he was certainly aware enough to know that the color blue was only a symptom for something else he couldn't diagnose. Something he didn't even want to think about, except it kept pelting him from every direction. No matter where he went, Erin's influence was already there. No matter where he looked, something there reminded him of her. Categorically, he denied interest, romance, love or anything like it. He wasn't even interested in her that way. Not now, not in the future. But she was the flame, he was the moth—a situation out of his control. One that made him grumpy as hell.

"It's only a color," Davion said. He was sitting cross-legged in the sand with a medical text spread out in front of him. Adam was sprawled in a red-and-orange-striped canvas cabana chair, his back to the hospital, more specifically to Erin, working with Davion on basic pharmacology.

"A color I'll have to look at every time I set foot out my door. Or look out the clinic window."

"I've heard people talking about it. They like it. Say it's different. The consensus is it's a nice color, better than the boring white." He grinned. "You're the only one around here who hates it."

"Well, everybody else can like it all they want but I'm

entitled to my opinion. And I may have to dock my boat to the south and live on it so I won't have to look at it." He wanted to glance over his shoulder, wanted to catch a glimpse of the progress. Or of Erin. A habit he had to stop, he thought as he purposely twisted in his chair and took one quick peek in that direction, trying to be sly about it then immediately chiding himself for doing so. Moth to the flame, damn it!

Davion chuckled. "You can look all you want, but she's not over there."

"Who?" he snapped. "And I'm not looking at anything."

"Erin. She's not over there right now. And I've seen you looking for her every time you think I'm not watching. But just so you know, I think she was going back to my mother's house to get her things. She's moving into one of the cottages, taking her belongings over there a few at a time. Tadeo's helping her."

"She takes my hospital *and* Tadeo!"

Grinning, Davion shook his head. "She's really getting to you, isn't she?"

"She's disrupting my routine. Bothering me."

"Seems to me she's been staying out of your way these past few days."

"Whose side are you on?" Adam snapped. "I've already lost Tadeo, but you, too?"

"I wasn't aware there were sides to choose. Oh, and just so you'll know, I promised to help her paint later on. *Blue*."

"*Et tu*, Davion?"

Davion chuckled. "Weren't we talking about beta-blockers?"

Beta-blockers—a class of drug used for the management of cardiac arrhythmias and cardio-protection after

a myocardial infarction…heart attack. Also used in treatment of hypertension. Which he was going to suffer if he
kept on fretting over Erin. "OK, beta-blocker or, as they're
sometimes referred to, beta-adrenergic blocking agents,
beta-adrenergic antagonists, or…"

"Beta antagonists," Davion supplied.

Adam nodded, and smiled in spite of his bad mood.
"Good. You've been doing your reading."

"Trying to. Sometimes it's not easy, with so many things
going on. And…" He frowned.

"And what?"

Davion shook his head. "Nothing."

"Tell me what it is, Davion."

"It's you. You're so…preoccupied. Sometimes I feel like
I'm interrupting you, maybe wasting your time."

Adam shut his eyes, drew in a deep breath. Davion was
right. He'd been fixed on the color blue, obsessed with
being grumpy, for three days now, almost to the exclusion
of everything else. "I'm not a very flexible person," he
admitted, knowing that was a huge understatement. He was
the proverbial immoveable force. Once he fixed on something, he didn't often budge. Which had brought about the
demise of his marriage, and he admitted that freely. At all
costs, he'd wanted to be a doctor in Jamaica. Had wanted
that since his student days when he'd come here with a
traveling medical group. And the cost of getting what he
wanted had been huge. But being inflexible…Davion was
too important to him to get caught up in that.

"Look, I'm sorry. None of this should be affecting you.
Right now you need to be concentrating on your studies so
you'll be ahead by the time you get to medical school. And
I think that scholarship will be coming through sooner than
we thought. So study fast." That's how he had to tame his
grumpiness. Look at that ugly blue building and think of

Davion in medical school because of it. Think about the kind of doctor Davion was going to be and the amazing things he would accomplish in his career. In a situation where *he* wasn't going to get everything he wanted, getting Davion to medical school made all his grumblings seem pretty damned lame. Which meant it was time to embrace blue and everything it stood for. For Davion's sake, even for his own sake. Fix himself on the things he could have, the things he could do, and let the rest of it go.

Drawing in a deep breath, Adam gritted his teeth toward his newfound determination. "So, beta-blockers reduce the effects of adrenaline and other stress hormones occurring in the body." He reeled off a list of some of the best examples on the market. "Any questions?"

Davion nodded. "When are you going to really fix things with Erin? Quit being so back and forth about the hospital and just get on with it? You need to, since you're going to be living right next door to each other. If you don't, you're going to need to take a beta-blocker yourself with the way you twist yourself into a knot every time she makes a change to the hospital."

"The one next door to me? That's the cabin she took?" he asked, trying to feign disinterest when all he could think about now was Erin stepping out her cottage door, standing on the porch, morning sun catching her hair… Damn, what an image! Moth to flame.

Davion nodded. "And she's going to paint it yellow, by the way."

"Yellow, not white?" *Next-door neighbors.* Of all the other cabins she owned, why that one? Why the one he would see every time he looked out his bedroom window into…her bedroom window? "OK, so I can live with yellow." But he was going to have to hang blinds in his window or plant a hedge row to obstruct the view.

Davion shut his book, picked it up, and stood. "Let's do this later, when you're not so preoccupied."

"I'm not preoccupied," he protested.

"In your list of beta-blockers, you left out carvedilol. That's one of the better examples, and I don't think you'd be forgetting it if you weren't so..." he grinned "...preoccupied." Davion sauntered off, in the direction of the clinic, humming a tune. Halfway there, he turned back, shouted to Adam, "It's showing on you. No hiding it." Then he disappeared into the clinic.

"Hiding what?" Erin asked, stepping up behind him.

Adam glanced up, drew in a sharp breath. "The fact that I hate blue."

"You're still fixed on that?" She stood above him, casting her shadow over his face.

"Trying not to be, but every time I look over there the color jumps out and bites me like it's a sand flea. You know it's there, hiding in the sand, waiting to get you. You don't really think that it will, though, but then, out of nowhere, you feel the bite, see the red blister pop up. It's not a major thing but it's annoying as hell."

"And I'm sorry about the sand flea, Coulson. That's why I'm here, hopefully to prevent you from getting bitten again. I'm taking a walk, trying to figure out where I can build a riding stable, and I wanted to apologize."

"Apologize for what?"

"For getting in your way. I should have come here and told you what I was planning before jumping in with both feet. You know, soften the blow. So I wanted to mention that I'm going to be putting in a riding stable, but not on this side of the property. Thought you might have an opinion on where it should go since you live so close. So it won't be another sand flea waiting to get you."

"If I give you my opinion, will you actually take it?"

She smiled. "Maybe. And maybe I should have asked for your opinion on some of the other things I'm doing since they will have an impact on you, too, and I'm sorry I didn't. But…when I saw the property advertised for sale, it was an answer to everything I'd hoped for, and from that moment on it was like I had to start pushing and push hard because I finally had my opportunity. This hospital is so important to me, Coulson. In one way or another, I've been planning it since I was a little girl. *The Algernon Glover Hospital for Children.* I learned a long time ago that if you want something, you shouldn't wait to go after it because, if you do, you might lose it. Or lose something more important while you're waiting. Anyway, I didn't want to lose this chance and I think my inclination is always to leap first, then look. But I should have been more respectful of your feelings because I do know that the beginning of my dream is the ending of yours, and for that I truly am sorry."

"Enough to paint the building white again?" he teased.

"You're so traditional."

"In most ways, I guess I am." The funny thing was, he'd never considered himself traditional, but now that Erin was pointing it out to him, he could see it. He could also see how being so traditional made him inflexible. Or boring. At least, in comparison to Erin. "And I'm the one who should be apologizing to you. You stepped into this deal with the expectation that I would be somewhat pleasant about it, and I've been nothing but a jerk. But I've meant it when I've told you it's not personal, because it's not, Red. I think your idea is admirable, though I still think this is the wrong place to put your dream."

"You don't know my dream, Coulson. It's so much more than…than a traditional hospital."

"You mean a hospital with a riding stable? I'll admit that's a twist I wouldn't have expected."

She nodded. "That's only a small part of it. I also want bicycle paths and a boat that's worthy of an ocean adventure. I want a beach where the children can go wading in the ocean and have a picnic. Maybe even a little petting zoo of sorts where the children can be involved with animals."

"It sounds more like you're creating a park, than a hospital."

"I am…*we* are, my father and me. This hospital isn't about being sick. It's a place where long-term, chronically ill children can come and be normal kids. They'll receive the best medical care, but they won't be confined to a typical institutional room and have only hospital corridors to wander through and starched white uniforms to look at. They'll have all of this…a place to play, a place to find peace of mind. A place to be children. Most of all, a place where being sick doesn't occupy every breath they take every last minute of the day. This hospital is a retreat as much as it is a hospital and I knew, the minute I saw the photos, this was the perfect place for it."

Well, he hadn't expected that. Not at all. And he did have to admit, at first impression, it sounded like a good idea. Made him feel quite sheepish for the way he'd been acting. "Why didn't you tell me all this before?" he asked.

"When I was a little girl…let's just say that I didn't have a normal life for a while, and every time I made a wish or had plans, and talked about something I wanted, it didn't happen. Didn't come true. After a while I learned that if I wanted something badly enough to keep it to myself. It's a silly eccentricity, I know. But I didn't want anything to jinx this because…" She paused, bit her lip, shut her eyes. Drew in a ragged breath. "Because it's important."

There was something more to it. He could see it, feel it. "Why, Red? Why is it so important. And urgent?"

"Because I want my father to see the bronze name plaque on the hospital. I want him to see what his influence has done."

All sorts of things were running through his mind, none with a good outcome. "Is he sick?" he asked, gently. "Your father, is he…?"

She shook her head. "Not sick. But going blind. Soon. When I was a little girl, my circumstances were difficult. My parents gave me up, and for a couple of years I was pretty much lost. When I met my father, he wasn't looking to adopt a little girl but over time that became his focus. Only it wasn't easy. In this modern age, there are still prejudices. Single man adopting a little girl. Black man adopting a white girl. He fought the system for two years, trying to make it happen, and our social worker, Mrs Meecham, kept telling him that she had faith it would. But my father, who's a bit of a pragmatist, and somewhat traditional, the way you are, kept telling her he'd have to see it to believe it, that he'd learned never to believe anything until he set eyes on it and saw it for himself. He had to *see* the adoption papers. And I know he has to see this hospital, see his name on it, because if he doesn't…" She cleared her throat. "He's sad right now. Sits in a dark room, doesn't get involved any more. He's helping do some of the administrative work for the hospital, making phone calls and arrangements, whatever he can do from his study, and I'd hoped that would make it real for him, but so far it hasn't. He's not involved the way he should be, the way I'd hoped he would be. And I'm afraid he's giving up, little by little."

"Erin, I…I don't know what to say."

She shook her head. "There's really nothing anybody can say. What's going to happen is going to happen, and we can't stop it. But I want, so badly, to make it better for him, the way he made it better for me. And your hospital…

when I saw it, that was the first time I ever truly believed I could do this while he still has his sight." Another tear slid down her cheek and this one she let fall. "He wouldn't come to Jamaica with me, and it scares me, because this is his home. He loves it here." She looked up at him, her eyes still glistening. "I've got to make it work, Coulson. For my father, but also for me. I want this as much as he does."

"You know you've just made me feel like the biggest cad on the face of the earth, don't you?"

"Because you wanted your hospital as much as I wanted mine? That doesn't make you a cad. It makes you... dedicated. That's a good thing, and I do understand the passion."

Another tear slipped down her cheek and this time he couldn't help himself. He pulled Erin into his arms and held her there. Stroked her hair as she laid her head against his chest. It was such an intimate moment. No kiss. No caress. Just Adam holding Erin through a tough moment, and disliking himself for being so rough on her, for hoping she'd fold and go home so he could capitalize on her failure. But now all of that was gone. And Davion was right. It was time he fixed this with Erin, once and for all. Time to move past it. "Know what, Red?"

"What?" she murmured, making no attempt to step away from him.

"Blue's not such a bad color. Would you mind, though, if I paint the shutters white?"

Davion's dulcet tones were on the verge of lulling her to sleep. Winding down the evening, sitting off in the corner listening to him sing and going over the budget for the planned renovations, was the perfect ending to a fairly good day. The architects had given her a promising report on how the hospital's interior refurbishment could be accomplished,

DIANNE DRAKE   97

she'd actually put three carpenters to work on the cottages she would use for guests of the hospital, visiting medics, parents... She wanted nice accommodations for everyone. That was all part of her plan. Nice ambiance. Everybody comfortable. Her big concern was the beach. In her estimation, it was essential because it had healing properties for the psyche. She remembered all those times her father would rent a cottage on the beach and take her. In her darkest, sickest hours, the beach had seemed so peaceful to her, and looking out over the vastness of the ocean so encouraging with the occasional ship off on the horizon, making its slow way someplace else. Erin had always wanted to be someplace else in those days—someplace where she wasn't sick. So she'd imagined herself on those ships, traveling to destinations unknown. When she got there, she'd be better, maybe even be cured.

Which was why she needed this beach for her children, because it offered so much hope. Yet she worried about the fact that it was not able to be attended all the time, which made it a danger. Adam, though, had stepped outside his traditional rut and suggested a fence around the hospital itself. Nothing with wire or cement, nothing that looked like it was meant to keep the children in. Rather something fun, asymmetrical, all the colors of the rainbow, except white. And she could see Coulson's fence in her mind. Amazing colors, maybe island scenes painted on the various pickets by the children. She could even imagine Coulson painting some of those pickets himself...blue.

"Good evening, ma'am Doc," a tiny voice from outside the open-air bar called, interrupting her thoughts.

She recognized Tadeo's voice. Was a little surprised to hear it as it was well after ten. But Coulson had said that Tadeo ran around all hours of the night.

"Ma'am Doc," he called again.

She glanced over at the bar, where Coulson was deep in a medical consult with an older man who seemed to be showing him a pair of very arthritic hands. It was an odd mixture of worlds, but it was her world now. "Good evening, Tadeo," she said, slipping out into the night. "Shouldn't you be home, in bed?"

He shrugged. Didn't say a word.

"Is something wrong?" Her thoughts went immediately to his heart murmur. "Are you sick?" Instinctively, she reached over, felt his forehead. Instincts of a mother, though, not a doctor.

"No," he said, reluctantly. "Not sick."

She pulled back her hand, and the doctor in her wanted to check his pulse. But she didn't, because this was a little boy who felt very guilty about something. Even in the dark shadows she could see it in his face. Hear it in the quavering of his voice. He wasn't sick. He was scared to death. "So, what's wrong?" she asked, trying to stay neutral for fear of scaring him off. They'd worked together earlier today. He'd helped her carry a few things from Trinique's cottage over to hers. And he was such a sweet boy. Very tentative, though. Afraid to say the wrong thing, do the wrong thing, take the wrong step. It broke her heart, because he was so eager to please and so afraid at the same time. Made her wonder even more about his treatment from Pabla. "You can tell me about it, Tadeo. I promise, we'll find a way to make it better."

"Can't make it better," he said, then pointed off in a vague direction, motioning for her to follow. No more explanation. He simply turned round and walked away, leaving Erin with no choice but to follow and wonder what was going on. All too soon, though, she knew. It was Adam's boat. Or what was left of it. More accurately, it was a smoldering pile of ashes, with a few red sparks still glowing. "What happened?" she asked Tadeo. When he didn't answer, she looked around, only to discover that he'd slipped away in the night.

Sighing, and suddenly dreading the task ahead of her, Erin turned and trudged back to Trinique's, where Davion had finished his last set of songs and Adam was sitting at one of the tables, feet propped up, quizzing him on the physiology of the lung. "I, um…I need to talk to you, Coulson." She glanced at Davion, who took the hint and immediately sprang to his feet.

"Looks serious," Adam said, not bothering yet to sit up.

"I think it is."

That caught his attention. He straightened, moved his feet to the floor, scooted to the edge of his chair, getting ready to go. "A patient?"

"Not any more."

"Someone die?" he asked, standing.

"Not someone. Some*thing*. It was your boat."

It took a minute for it to sink in. Then, "My boat?"

She nodded. "I'm sorry. But by the time I got there it was too late. It was…"

"My boat?" he sputtered, still not comprehending. "*Stella*?"

"Burned up. Nothing to be salvaged, at least as far as I could tell. I didn't get too close because it was still smoldering, but it looked like a total loss."

"You're sure it was *my* boat?"

"Tadeo took me there. So I'm assuming—"

He dashed past her before she could finish. Hung up the Closed sign and ran out the door, then headed to the beach. Loss was loss, and Erin knew the pain of it. She wasn't sure what his attachment to the boat was, but it was substantial, and she knew she should go after him. But she waited for a moment to tell Davion, who was standing at the far end of the hut.

"His boat caught fire," she said. "Total loss."

"That's not good. He loves that boat, probably more than he's ever loved anybody in his life, but his grandpa."

"It was a connection to his grandfather?"

Davion nodded. "That, and the property here he bought with the inheritance from his grandpa."

Erin sucked in a sharp breath. "So now…"

"That's it. Half the property is gone, along with the boat. As long as he had his boat, he was OK. But this…" He shrugged. "It's going to be hard on him. Probably harder than selling his property."

Erin swallowed back a hard lump. "I think I'd better go…"

"He'll want to be alone," Davion warned.

"Maybe so." But she still had to go. Because right now Coulson was standing out there on that beach, feeling like he had nothing left in the world. The least she could do was let him know he had a friend.

"I'm really sorry about this, Coulson," she said, keeping her distance. In the moonlight, she saw his slumped shoulders, saw the defeated stance. "Davion told me what it meant to you, and I'm truly sorry."

"Me too," he said, his voice thick.

"I think it might have been Tadeo. He was pretty upset when he came to get me, and—"

Coulson shook his head, extended his hand to wave her off. "He wasn't hurt, was he?"

"I don't think so, but I don't know. He ran away too fast, and I didn't think to ask him."

He turned to face her. "Then I'll go and find him. He may have suffered some burns, and I doubt if he'd tell me after this."

"Maybe, in the morning, when you can see the boat better—"

"Gone is gone, Red. You really mess up your head if you hang on to false hope, and *Stella* is a pile of false hope now. But thanks for trying to cheer me up."

She stepped closer. Close enough that the moon accented the pain on his face. "Look, I'll go find Tadeo. Right now I doubt if he'd let you get anywhere near him. He's probably scared to death that…"

"That I'll be angry?"

"That you'll hate him, or you'll never want to see him again. When you think you're going to be rejected…it's like all this craziness goes on around you, and everyone you know is in on it. Everything you do causes it. When you're being rejected by someone you love, that's all there is in your life and it's the worst feeling, the worst kind of dread you can imagine. That's what Tadeo is going through right now. Total loss. I mean, I never burned a boat, but I know how he's feeling so, please, let me go and find him."

"Bring him back to the clinic, if you can."

"Will you talk to him?"

"I have to, don't I? Don't know what to say yet."

She squeezed his arm. "You'll know what to say when the time comes."

"Just find him. I'm worried."

"Are you going to be OK, Coulson?" He seemed so… sad. Sad, like her father was, and her heart ached for both her dad and for the man standing in front of her.

"Do you care, Red? After the way I've acted, do you really care?"

"Yeah, I suppose I do. Don't ask me why, but I do." The truth was, she cared more than she wanted to let on, and she wasn't even going to bother denying it. To Coulson she would, but to herself…what was the point? She did care and there was no getting around it. The only thing was, she couldn't let those feelings get in the way. And that thought was what sent her off into the night, looking for Tadeo. She was there for reasons other than involvement and personal feelings. Her goal was clear, even if the edges were becoming a little fuzzy. As long as fuzzy didn't turn into fully frayed, she'd be fine. But she had an idea that Coulson could cause a whole lot of fraying. Which was why she was glad to run off into the night…alone. There was no time in her life for fraying of any kind.

CHAPTER SIX

"You people leave him alone!" Pabla Reyes yelled at Erin.

"I just wanted to make sure he's not hurt. Is he here?" Judging from the expression on the woman's face, that was a question she couldn't answer because she didn't know. Erin stepped back from the door, expecting a slam in the face, and had moved just in the nick of time, as that's exactly what the woman did. She slammed the door so hard it rattled the front window. So, the question was, if Tadeo wasn't home...and Erin was pretty sure he was not...where else would he go at this time of night? It was going on to midnight now, much too late for an eight-year-old to be out alone, running around.

Stepping off the wooden stoop, she stood in the dirt for a moment, listening to the night sounds. Nothing but silence, and the night calls from a few lonely animals seeking companionship. "No sign," she said to Coulson, who was on his way up the path to the Reyes house. "Pabla wasn't cooperative, and I don't think she knows where he is." She paused, studying his strong physique in the moonlight. Just the sight of him took her breath away, and she was getting used to that. Too used to it, in fact. Enjoying it too much. Honestly, Adam Coulson was the first man she'd ever really noticed in *that* way. Part of the reason had been the fear of the cancer returning someday, and the other part of the reason…she didn't trust relationships, except the one with her father. He'd adopted her when she'd been sick, but other than her father nobody else had ever stayed and, early into her disease, she'd learned not to expect them to. Cancer was ugly. It was a harbinger, a reminder, a glimpse nobody wanted to take.

So, no, she didn't trust relationships, and Adam had given her no real reason to trust him.

Except she did. More than that, her feelings seemed to be straying a little further than trust, and the tingles running up and down her arms right now were the tangible proof of that. Good thing she had the sense to know she couldn't do anything about it. Not that he'd tried anything. Or so much as hinted at it.

"Well, I went back to Trinique's, couldn't find him there. Thought he might be at the clinic, but he wasn't. Checked back around the boat. No luck there either."

"Would he have run away?" she asked, trying not to think about Tadeo out there alone in the jungle at that time of night. He was a resourceful little boy, though, well at home in his surroundings. So she shouldn't be worried. But she couldn't help herself. She was, and it was growing by the minute.

"He's independent. I don't think he realizes that boys his age have limitations so, yes, he could have run. But he's a good kid. I think he's more inclined to face me at some point and see if he can make good. Or, at the very least, apologize."

"But what will he do if he thinks you've totally turned against him? He knows you loved that boat, Coulson. And I believe he loved it probably as much as you did. For the same reason you did—it tied him to someone important to him. Think about it. What would you have done, when you were his age, if you'd destroyed it?"

"Felt like the whole world had turned against me. Been scared to death. Wanted to crawl in a hole somewhere and never come out. Or run away."

"Exactly. He's eight, probably a little afraid of the dark, so I don't think he's gone too far from his comfort zone, *yet*. But I have an idea that if we don't find him tonight, he'll be gone by tomorrow."

"Then I'll look until I find him," Adam said.

"*We…we'll* look until we find him." She held out her hand to Adam, and he took it.

"You're too nice to me, Red. I don't deserve it, after the way I've acted."

"You're right. I *am* too nice to you, and you don't deserve it. But we're neighbors. You're not going anywhere, I'm not going anywhere, so getting along makes it easier. Otherwise we'd have to build a real fence between our properties, and I like the view on your side." More than she would admit to him.

He chuckled. "You beat everything. Do you know that?"

"Is that a compliment?"

"It just might be."

Hand in hand, they walked down the dark path, looking for Tadeo, calling his name. Occasionally they separated, went off in different directions to search. But always came back together in a matter of a minute or two. And each time the way her hand slipped so naturally into his…it felt right to him. Such a simple thing, yet such a significant one. She was definitely getting to him. And as Davion had suggested, that's why he'd been grumpy so much lately. Fundamentally, he didn't want to be gotten. But Erin was so…good. Sexy as hell, a genuine femme fatale the way she attracted him, and he didn't think she even knew she had it in her. She did, though. More than that, she had such strength, such a sense of purpose, which he found almost as sexy as the rest of her.

He'd given up, a long time ago, thinking there could be a complete package. Every woman fell short in some way. Then there was Erin, who totally wiped that idea out of his mind. And, damn, he wished he could do something about it, more than hold her hand. But they were going to spend a long time here together, living next door to each other, working, maybe not together but in parallel, so what if he did advance, and she retreated? Or what would happen if they got together in some way other than professional, and it didn't work out?

He wasn't inclined to take the risk because he knew how those risks turned out. He'd done it before. Married the person he'd thought would share his dream, even though, when he looked back on those days, he truly hadn't seen any evidence of that in Janice. Not a speck. Maybe he had seen only what he'd wanted to see. Who knew? But he'd taken that risk anyway and had ended up down and almost out. So, not this time. No more risks. He'd come here for a reason, stayed here for a reason, forfeited his marriage for that very same reason, and he didn't want that boat rocked in any way. Of course, a superstitious man might have read something into that boat actually burning. But he wasn't a superstitious man. Wasn't a risk-taking man either.

So, for Erin and him it had to be friendship. That's all there was to it. To maintain their relationship in the long-term, the only thing it could be was camaraderie based on professional respect. Something he truly regretted, though, because the thoughts in his mind... Anyway, they both had goals, and that's what he had to remember, *all the time*. He wanted to succeed in his own goals but, as much as he wanted what he wanted, he also wanted Erin to have success in her goals, too.

"Look," he said, reluctantly dropping her hand and stepping away from her. "He might have gotten into one of your buildings. It's not where he would have normally gone, but these aren't normal circumstances."

"Nothing is locked up," she said. "It would be easy for him to hide there."

"Then why don't you take the main building and I'll go look in the outbuildings? If we don't find him in any of those…I think we're going to have to wake Davion and a few of the locals and start a real search." He held out a flashlight to her. "It's not much, but it will help. You take the shorter way and I'll take the other path around, and unless he's actually gone off into the trees somewhere, that will cover us between here and the hospital compound."

Erin nodded then, without another word, turned and ran in the direction of her hospital. In the dim light coming from the Reyes cottage, he watched her on the path until she was gone then took the alternate route, glad he didn't have to watch her run…watch her crazy, wild hair fly in the breeze, watch legs he wanted wrapped around him moving gracefully in long strides, watch her hips swaying…

Definitely he needed a different path. In more ways than one.

"Tadeo," she called into the darkness. She hadn't been here at night and, on entering the main ward after a quick check of the private rooms, she was attacked by a galloping case of goosebumps. It wasn't that she was frightened by the dark, because she wasn't. But this room…it seemed so large, so empty, and the purpose of everything she wanted to accomplish here suddenly came alive. During the day, this was a hospital. It looked like one, would function as one. But now, at night…when she'd been young, nights had always been the worst. Dark, barren hours with nothing to do but think, or be afraid. The nights had terrified her, not the darkness so much as the emptiness, especially when she'd been in one of her sicker cycles. Daylight always made things better, though. It brought new hope and that's what she wanted here. New hope.

Her kids weren't ever going to be in the dark, Erin decided. After the large ward was turned into separate rooms, she would paint luminescent stars on all the ceilings, make sure there were night-lights everywhere. No total darkness. Not for her kids. "Are you in here, Tadeo? You're not in trouble, Adam's not angry about his boat, but he's very worried about you. We're both worried. Afraid you may have gotten hurt…or burned. Tadeo?"

She held still, listened. Didn't hear so much as a scrape on the wooden floor or the rustle of someone shifting positions nearby. Or the sound of panicked little breaths either. But the obvious lack of anybody there didn't stop her from looking, from walking up the center aisle and shining the wavering beam from the light on each and every bed, then down underneath. Sixteen beds examined, and no Tadeo. He wasn't in the tiny exam room at the end, not in the room set aside for staff, or even the room she'd designated to be her surgery. Not in the supply closet either. Nowhere.

On that discouraging note, she headed back to the front door, keeping her fingers crossed that Coulson was having better luck. Just at the front, though, in the tiny reception area, she flashed her light on a built-in closet, meant for hanging jackets, maybe lab coats. It was barely more than the size of a modest locker, but she opened the door anyway and there, huddled in a ball at the bottom, was Tadeo. His big brown eyes wide, he simply stared up at her, didn't say a word.

"We all make mistakes," she said, holding out her hand to him. "I'm sure you were only trying to help Adam with his boat, and you didn't mean for the fire to happen. He knows it was an accident, Tadeo."

"It was dark," he sniffled, not taking her hand, not making a move to come out. "I was trying to get ready to varnish. Doing some more sanding."

"And you lit a fire to see by? Is that what happened?"

He nodded. "In the lantern."

"Then accidentally knocked it over."

"I tried to stop it," he said, as the tears started to slide down his face. "Tried hitting it with some of the rags and stomping on it. But the fire got so big."

"Where were you burned, Tadeo?" she asked gently, instinctively knowing that he had been.

He shrugged.

"Can I see where you were burned? It's got to hurt awfully bad, doesn't it? Maybe I can find something to make it feel better."

Finally, he nodded, and held out both hands. The insides were burned, from his palms to his fingers. Red, splotchy, already blistering in places. The poor child had been too frightened to get help and the pain had to be terrible for him.

"Look, Tadeo, I need you to come out of the closet so I can help you."

"He's going to hate me," Tadeo whispered, still resisting her.

"He doesn't hate you. In fact, he's out looking for you right now because he was afraid you might have got burned, and he wants to take care of you." She thought that might draw him out when, in fact, it caused him to draw in on himself even more. "How about if I take you over to the clinic and take care of your burns myself, then we don't even tell him about it? Would that be OK?"

A tentative nod was all that Tadeo mustered, but it was enough to cause Erin to bend down and gently tug Tadeo from the floor of the closet then bundle him up in her arms and head for the door. "You're almost as tall as I am," she said, struggling not so much from Tadeo's weight but from the awkwardness of carrying a larger child without hurting him any further than he was already. At the front door, she simply kicked it open then descended the two steps—steps she was going to turn into a ramp soon. Halfway across the compound's central yard, she saw Coulson step out of one of the cabins and shine his light directly on her. She shook her head at him when he started to run toward her then shook her head more vigorously as he continued his approach. The second warning stopped him, but not for long as he fell into step quite a way behind her, and followed her to his clinic. Once there, he ran to the back door, opened it and went immediately to open the front door for her. But he stepped behind the door as she entered carrying Tadeo, so Tadeo wouldn't see him there.

He was a man who truly loved this child. There was no hiding it. And there was no hiding his anguish. The kind of man she could love, if she was willing to take that step… someday.

"It's going to hurt a little bit," she explained to the boy, who was nestled against her so tightly it made walking difficult. The easiest thing would have been to hand the boy over to Coulson, but Tadeo wasn't ready for that yet. Wasn't ready to face the person she believed he cared about more than anybody in the world. "But I'm going to give you something that will make you feel better."

In the first tiny exam she came to, Erin laid Tadeo on the table, turned on the light then took a good look at the burns for the first time. Second degree, but not as bad as they could have been. "I need to go and get some bandages," she told him. "You stay here, don't move around too much, OK?"

Tadeo nodded bravely, but the quiver to his bottom lip told her his bravery had just about run out.

One step into the hall and Coulson pulled her all the way across, into the other exam room. "How is he?" he choked, his voice so low she could barely hear him.

"Scared to death. With second-degree burns on both his hands."

"Does he need to go to the hospital?"

"No. I can take care of it here. And he's not ready to face you yet, Coulson. I'm sorry. He's really frightened, and I tried reassuring him that you're not angry, but he's a stubborn little boy and he doesn't want to see you...right now." She gave his arm a supportive squeeze. "But he will when he's feeling better. Just give it some time."

"Pabla needs to know," Coulson said.

"Will she care?" Erin didn't think she would, which made her heart ache all the more for Tadeo.

"I'm going to roust out Davion and send him over here to help you while I go and confront...*tell* her what happened."

"Could Davion do that?"

"Because you think I'll say something I shouldn't?"

"Because you're too emotionally involved and, yes, I do think you'll say something you shouldn't. Not that Pabla doesn't deserve it."

"I'll be fine. On my good behavior because Tadeo needs that from me."

"Then I'll take you at your word, Coulson, but would you get me some water before you go? I want to cool down his hands first, before anybody does anything else."

"Back in a minute," Coulson said, then bolted out the door like a man running for his life. Three minutes later, while she was still gathering supplies, Davion appeared with a bucket of water.

"He decided to go and have a talk with Miss Reyes right away, while he was still relatively calm." He handed the bucket to Erin. "He's pretty mad about this...not the boat but about how she doesn't pay attention to Tadeo, and he doesn't want to make things worse for the boy. Anyway, can I help you? I've never treated anything other than a first-degree burn before, but I can do whatever you need."

"I'd love your help, Davion." In spite of his promise to her, Erin didn't imagine Coulson was going to be too amiable in his confrontation with Pabla Reyes. But maybe that was OK, because Tadeo needed someone on his side, someone to fight for him. Someone to be fierce. Coulson, it seemed, was that someone, and it did her heart good to see the depth of his emotion for the boy. In Tadeo's life, that would make a difference. It would in Coulson's life, too.

"If the second-degree burn is no larger than seven or eight centimeters in diameter, treat it as you would a minor burn. Cool it, cover it, control the pain. Luckily, Tadeo's small hands won't accommodate anything larger than seven centimeters, so we're in luck. But the exception to that is if the burn area is larger, or it's on the patient's hands, feet, face, groin or buttocks, or even over a major joint. Then it has to be treated like it's a major burn. In other words, urgent care."

"So, Tadeo's a pretty lucky kid," Davion replied, more for Tadeo's sake than anything else.

"Tadeo's very lucky. And to prove it, he's going to get some of the very best bandages I've ever done." She smiled at Tadeo, who looked so scared it broke her heart. Actually, these weren't going to be easy wounds to manage, given his age and home circumstances, and she had an idea Tadeo understood that. "Now, there are several ways to cool a burn, but the first thing to remember is that you can never let a burn come into contact with ice. That can cause further damage, often tears the skin that's still intact. But you can hold the burned area under cool running water for about fifteen minutes, which isn't practical for us as the sink is too high for Tadeo to reach. So, do you know any other method of treatment?" she asked, feeling, for a moment, like she was Davion's teacher. A little bit of Coulson rubbing off on her, she supposed.

"Cold compress. Or you can immerse the wound in cool water…like in a bucket. Sterile water's the best, if you have it, which we don't. However you do it, though, the reason is to reduce the swelling that's going on by conducting the heat away from the skin." He grinned. "Adam has taught me well."

"Don't underestimate your own ability, Davion. You have a gift for medicine." She grabbed a stack of sterile gauze pads from the supply shelf, as well as a stack of wash rags.

"And I'll be going to medical school in a few months."

Once organized, she began to dip the rags in the water. "I didn't know it was going to be so soon."

"I was expecting to wait for a while, but Adam sold his hospital to get me there before I'm an old man. He's been saying he applied for a scholarship for me, and he thinks I don't know he's the one going to pay most of my way. I've felt bad that he had to sell his hospital, but he did it before I knew what he was doing. So, because of what he's done, I'm going to make sure he's proud of me."

"Don't feel bad that he sold his hospital, Davion. When

you love someone, you want to make the sacrifices. That's the best kind of life anybody can live, and even though he's grumpy about it, that's the kind of life Coulson lives, or lived, until I showed up. And I know for a fact that he's very proud of you. Now, lay the compresses gently on Tadeo's hands then switch the compress as soon as you feel it turning warm. You'll be able to feel the heat from his burns radiating out. Keep applying them while I go and find something to take the edge off his pain. You wouldn't happen to know what kind of pain medicine Coulson has on hand, would you?"

"Ibuprofen. In the back room, not locked up."

She was barely in the hall when Coulson came running, breathless, straight at her. "How is he?"

"Davion's applying cold compresses right now, and I'm on my way to find ibuprofen. Tadeo's not saying anything, being quite a little trouper, though. And Pabla?"

"Said she didn't care, that if he got burned it was his own fault. She's not going to pay for the treatment, by the way."

Erin smiled. "Why am I not surprised?" She thought about Coulson and his two "sons" for a moment. Davion and Tadeo. They were lucky with Coulson the way she'd been lucky with her father. "Look, let me get the ibuprofen..."

No sooner had she spoken the words then Adam dashed off. Back in ten seconds, he held out the bottle. "He likes fruit juice. I don't have any here, but I've got some in my cottage."

She imagined he kept it there for Tadeo. Of course he would.

"He's going to be fine," Erin said, sitting down next to Adam in his clinic's waiting room. He looked as on edge as any one person could look, which concerned her because none of this was his fault, but he was taking the blame for it anyway. "Davion's with him now, said he'd sit with him for a while. The pain meds have taken off enough of the edge of Tadeo's pain that I think he'll sleep comfortably for the rest of the night. And, Coulson, I really am sorry about your boat."

"It was just a damn bunch of wood. No big deal."

She knew it was, though. "Look, why don't I relieve Davion…and you? Then you can get some sleep."

"Sleep?"

"You know, where you shut your eyes, probably snore…"

"I don't snore," he snapped, then immediately shut his eyes, dropped his head back on the wall and let out a long, exasperated breath. "Look, Red. I'm sorry. I shouldn't have—"

"You lost something important," she interrupted. "You're entitled to your feelings."

"It was a boat. I still have the memories. But what I may have lost is Tadeo, and that's…" He shook his head. "That's what's got me madder than hell. An eight-year-old kid needs guidance, needs his mother, or in this case his guardian, to look after him. Tadeo doesn't have that and I don't know how to make it better for him."

"Maybe you can't," she said gently. "Not everything can be fixed, and maybe Tadeo's situation is one of them. I'm mean, we have limitations, Coulson. We can treat his burns, we can even treat his heart murmur, but anything else is overstepping ethical bounds. And I know that's hard for you to accept. But what scares me for Tadeo right now is that because Pabla is so hostile to us, she'll take it out on him." She stood. "Look, I'm going back to my cottage, grab a pillow, change my clothes, and come back. Davion can go home…he needs his rest as much as you do as he's getting ready for medical school. And, in the mean time, this doctor is prescribing bed rest for the other doctor. No arguments."

"I'm fine," Davion said from the door to the exam room. "I've got some reading to do, and I'm good to go for the night. You two go on, and if I need anything, I'll call." He grinned. "We may not have cell phones out here, but I think I can manage a regular phone."

"Point taken," Coulson said, standing. "I'll relieve you in three hours. That OK?"

"Take four," Davion said. "You look like hell."

"He has a way with words," Coulson said, following Erin out the door.

"Right's right, Coulson. You do look like hell. You take six hours, and I'll relieve Davion in three. Doctor's orders…again." She headed off toward Trinique's cottage, but Coulson reached out, grabbed her arm and stopped her.

"Where are you going?"

"My cottage isn't ready to live in yet. I'll probably stay at Trinique's another day or so, until I can get to Port Wallace and buy a few necessities. You know, towels, bath soap, a bed…"

"Take my bed," he said.

"What?"

"Trinique's is too far to walk at this time of the night."

"And you don't have to."

"Yes, I do. And I don't want to. So bunk with me tonight."

"Well, isn't that just the nicest offer I've ever had to spend the night with a man?" she teased. "Like Davion, you seem to have a way with words, too."

"Do you always do that, Red?"

"What?"

"Argue, for the sake of arguing. I'm tired, I've had a bad day, I don't want to walk all the way over to Trinique's, and here you are, standing out here in the middle of the night, arguing with me, which is preventing me from following my doctor's orders to get some sleep. As a doctor yourself, you should know the value of a good, cooperative patient."

"OK, OK, you've made your point. Your cabin. But you get the bed. I'll take the... What else do you have to sleep on?"

"The floor."

"Fine. Floor is good."

"I get lizards. And spiders. Non-poisonous variety." He let go of the grasp on her arm yet held on as they started to walk, like lovers strolling arm in arm.

"Then you get the floor."

Any other time, any other situation, and this could have been a nice, romantic stroll. But it wasn't, and she had to keep reminding herself of that every step of the way over to his cabin. Once inside, she was amazed by the sparseness...barely any furniture, practically no comforts. Three rooms. Bedroom, a combination living room and kitchen, and a bathroom. And, truly, there was only one place to sleep. A big double bed that sank in toward the middle and a threadbare rug on the floor in the living room/kitchen combo. No door separating the two rooms either. Thank heavens there was a door on the bathroom. "I'm holding you to your word, Coulson," she said, kicking off her shoes once she'd entered the bedroom.

"Which word is that?" he said, grabbing a spare pillow from his bed.

"That you don't snore."

"Do you?" he asked.

"Guess you're about to find out, aren't you?"

"Look, Red…what you did for Tadeo tonight…"

Even from the next room she heard his deep sigh. It would catch up to him in the morning…Tadeo's condition, the demise of *Stella*. It wasn't going to be a very good day for Dr Adam Coulson, and there wasn't a thing she could do about it. "Just go to sleep. We both need our rest." Her in a marginally comfy bed, him with the spiders and lizards. Well, the sleepover had been his idea after all.

Sleep didn't take over for at least an hour…a long, restless hour in which her mind was filled with so many things. All she could do was toss and turn and hope all the activity would wear her out. But it didn't, and she thought about her hospital, her father…most of all, she thought about the man sleeping in the very next room. Pictured him bare-chested. Hair mussed. Stubble on his face. Definitely an image that lost her some sleep.

CHAPTER SEVEN

COULSON'S shower was maybe the best thing that had happened to her since she'd come to Regina. There was a shower in Trinique's cottage, but all it would give was a cold trickle that was in scant supply...occasionally. While the pipes creaked and groaned. But this...this was wonderful. Designer showerhead, warm water that sprayed rather than drizzled. The feeling that she could take her time and enjoy this rather than jump in and right back out. Funny how she'd always taken her showers back home for granted. Like she had her good stethoscope or abundant medical supplies at her fingertips when she'd needed them. Despite the differences, though, she liked Regina. And not just because it was where her hospital would open its doors. She liked the people, liked the lifestyle...liked Coulson. He was a diamond in the rough. Everything good was underneath the unpolished exterior while the unpolished exterior itself wasn't so bad.

"Save me some hot water," he yelled through the door.

"You're supposed to be sleeping. Didn't I prescribe six hours of sleep for you?"

"You did, but how can you expect me to sleep with all the racket you're making? And just so you know, it takes a good two hours before the water heater will give hot water again."

The thought of him joining her to conserve water flitted through her mind, sending a wave of heat through her body. Where had that come from? They were colleagues, even friends, she told herself. He was acting as platonically as any man could act toward a woman. Oh, there were some nice gestures, but more from protectiveness than anything else. At least, that's the only way she could describe it. Even last night, when she'd half expected him to take up one side of the bed, he'd preferred to sleep with the lizards. Which told her exactly what her status was with him.

"You'll get your hot water later, after you've slept three more hours," she yelled back, while she lathered her hair with shampoo bearing the same lime scent she'd smelled on him. Nice. So nice that another fantasy popped in. One where she smelled of his lime, not from shampooing but from close physical contact. Even nicer. "So, go back to bed, and take the bed!" Hard words to say because she could have used another couple of hours there. But duty called. And she really was anxious to go and check on Tadeo. Also to get away from some awfully dangerous fantasies.

Stepping out of the shower nearly twenty minutes later, she looked for a towel. Couldn't find one. Not a clean one, not even a used one. Nothing on the shelf, nothing hanging on the hook on the door. Which meant her options were to stand there and drip-dry, yell for Coulson, or... No way she'd tiptoe out there dripping wet and naked, looking for a towel. So she opted to call for him or, at least whisper for him in the hope he was still awake. If he wasn't...

Peeking out, she didn't see him. Didn't see a light on in the opening to the bedroom either. Maybe he'd gone to sleep. And...left his bedsheet over the back of the chair, mere inches out of her reach. Saw it, reached out for it, couldn't get it. So, braving the emptiness, she opened the door all the way, took one dart at the sheet and almost made it all the way back into the bathroom when…

"You could have asked," he said, his voice emanating from somewhere within that room. From the dark.

She yanked the sheet up around her. "I didn't want to wake you up."

"You didn't. I ran over to check on Tadeo. Can you imagine how surprised I was when I came back to my cabin, stepped through the door, and saw, well…I suppose the best way I could describe it is heaven."

Heaven? Is that what he really thought? Rather than being embarrassed, she was flattered. "I needed a towel. You didn't have one."

"Actually, I do. I have…one. Didn't think you'd want to use that, so I grabbed one from the clinic when I was over there."

She could see his silhouette in the dark now, see that he was holding the towel straight out in front of him. So now her options were simple. March across the room, wrapped up in his sheet, and grab the towel from his hand. Or wait for him to bring it to her. "May I have it?"

"Trust me, I don't think you need it."

A raspy sigh accented the end of his words, and she felt her skin tingle all over. "I…I need to get dried so I can go and relieve Davion."

"Davion's fine. He said he'll be good until morning. Which means we get three more hours here…together." He crossed the room slowly, the wooden boards squeaking under his weight. Prolonged steps, deliberate. Almost like each and every one was thought out. "But since I'm going to have three more hours with that sheet you're getting wet…"

"I'm going to take over for Davion. He may be fine, but he needs to rest so he can study for his exam. So just give me the towel, Coulson. Let me get dried and dressed, and get this awkward moment over with."

"I'm not awkward. In fact, I'm grateful."

"For what?" She stepped forward and grabbed the towel he was finally extending to her.

"Well, I didn't see much. Just a glimpse. And it *was* dark in here, damn it. What I wouldn't have given for a little light on the subject… Oh, and by the way, was that a little tattoo on your—?"

"A birthmark," she said. "And how could you see that in the dark, all the way across the room?"

"Actually, I couldn't. It's was just a particular fantasy of mine." He chuckled. "But now I have another fantasy."

"You're a doctor, for heaven's sake! Act like one!"

"And you're a very sexy lady who's spending the night in my bed and showering in my shower. That's *definitely* not a doctor's observation, Red." He chuckled. "Or the other argument I could use here is that doctors are people, too. And at this moment I'm feeling particularly *people-ish*."

"*People-ish*?"

He nodded. "No doctor in me anywhere right now. So that leaves…"

"People-ish." He always did that. Always twisted the situation into whatever he wanted, and she was so darned captivated or charmed or whatever it was called when someone fell under a spell that she'd just stood there and let him. For heaven's sake! This was crazy. *She* was crazy. And the only way she was going to find her sanity was to get away from him. So that's what she did. She retreated into the bathroom to finish drying and get dressed. And concentrate on other things. Like… "Do you have a comb or a hairbrush in here?" she asked, dreading the task of working the tangles from her hair. She loved her hair. But it was a chore.

"Check the cabinet over the sink. If it's not there, I might have to come in and help you look for it."

She chuckled. He was incorrigible. Absolutely incorrigible, and she liked that about him. It gave him character. Jagged in places, but nice.

Opening the cabinet, she stood back and took stock of the things that were, quintessentially, Coulson. *His* deodorant, *his* toothbrush, *his* hairbrush, *his* razor—an old-fashioned one with disposable blades, not the new, plastic, throw-away type. There were also several more bottles of lime-scented shampoo. Attached to one was a thank-you note for his medical services. Rather than money, he accepted shampoo. Quintessentially Coulson again. A hard lump stuck in her throat as it struck her what a good man he was. But it also struck her how entirely removed he was. He lived alone, subsisted on the barest necessities in an isolated little stretch of the world. By design. It was Adam Coulson and…nobody. And there was nothing to suggest that he wanted somebody else there with him in any significant way. Not even a second towel. It was like he reached out, but never quite touched.

Most of *her* life, her father had accused her of keeping to herself. It was true. She had, and still did so much of the time. But not like this. Not to the point of quarantine, and that's how Coulson seemed to her. Quarantined.

Who knew? Maybe it was just easier for him that way. Maybe he'd made peace with his solitary self, and everything was good for him.

Still, he was such a caring man, and to care as deeply as he did meant to step outside yourself. Which he did. But then, when anybody got too near except, maybe Tadeo and Davion, he retreated. Made her wonder why. Made her wonder what, in his past, had made him so…afraid to care.

Was it his failed marriage? Had he given his heart and had it handed back to him brutally?

Grabbing the brush, she decided to exit the bathroom and all the little Coulson things surrounding her. The next ordeal was probably going to take a good ten minutes, and brushing the tangles outside, on the porch, seemed a good idea, considering how his impersonal toiletries seemed to set off her fantasies as much as anything else did. And that way Coulson could go back to sleep undisturbed while she headed over to the clinic to relieve Davion as soon as she was presentable.

Outside, she took a seat on a bench and inhaled the crisp island air. The nights here were so amazing. So absolutely pure. The darkness had a life of its own going on, with all sorts of little creatures darting in and out of the bushes. Yet in their night calls…the calls meant to find their mates… there was such hope. And tranquility. The hope was what she liked best, because it transcended into the hope that always stirred her. Hope that somewhere, sometime, she too would find her…true love. "Why are you out here, Coulson?" she asked, when the screen door behind her banged shut, shattering her solitude.

"To keep you company. To watch that mess on top of your head transform into a miracle."

She started the methodical brushing, one small section at a time. "It's not a big deal," she said, then winced as one tangle particularly hurt. "Normally, I use a cream rinse then I brush it immediately after I shower so the tangles don't…"

"Embed themselves?"

"They don't embed, Coulson." Another snarl caught, and she struggled to pull the brush through without actually breaking her hair.

"You could cut it short. Out here, that might be more practical."

"I don't want it—Ouch!" This time the brush was caught up. Twisted in tightly, just below her neck. "Look, I don't need an audience, OK? Go back to bed. Get some sleep. Let me do this by myself."

"With all the screaming going on out here, I won't be able to go to sleep."

"I'm not screaming."

"But you will be if you keep it up." He pulled her fingers off the hairbrush, took it away from her and gently untangled the snarl. He didn't give the brush back, though, when that tangle was set free. Rather, he started brushing her hair.

"What are you doing?" she asked, wanting her words to sound like a growl and realizing that they sounded more like a contented purr.

"Saving you the aggravation. So just sit there, relax, don't complain."

"I don't always complain." And she certainly wasn't going to complain about the tingles he was causing, not just on her scalp but everywhere else. "Only when I have to…" Definitely a purr now. This was wonderful. So intimate. So…luxurious. So surprising, because she was protective of her hair. *Overprotective* was probably a better way to describe it as she never let anybody touch it except for an occasional trim, and then, only by a select few stylists. And having Coulson brushing it this way for her, and her not stopping him from doing it, was unsettling in ways she wasn't prepared to decipher. Normally she recoiled when people touched her hair…and people did like to touch it. But she hated that. Would always cringe then back away politely. Yet there was *nothing* about Coulson's touch that made her want to recoil or back away. In fact, she loved having him touch her hair. Loved it so much she finally relaxed a little with a contented sigh.

"Enjoying this, Red?"

"Maybe." More than she would admit to him, or even to herself.

He chuckled. "Well, coming from you, I'll take that to be a big, resounding *yes*."

It was. She just wasn't going to tell him so.

"But you're not easy with it, are you? Your shoulders are still pretty tense, your neck is stiff. You've scooted forward to the edge of the bench, like you're getting ready to run. So, do I make you nervous, Red? Is it because I saw your—?"

"You saw my rear end, Coulson. At least, I'm assuming that's all you saw. And, no, that doesn't make me nervous." Quite that opposite, actually. "But don't count on ever seeing it again."

"Than I shall thank you for the opportunity and cherish the memory. Let it live on in my fantasies for years… decades to come."

In spite of herself, she laughed. And finally relaxed all the way.

"See, now, isn't that better?" he asked, as the brush finally began to glide more easily through her hair. "Even your hair's beginning to relax."

"Like it could."

"Well, I've got to admit, the first thing I noticed about you was your hair."

"The first thing? Are you sure? Because I thought it was my…money."

"OK, maybe the second…or third thing. And money always gets my attention, especially when someone's handing it over to me. But your hair was definitely in my top-five first observances because I figured that if you stayed here for long, you'd cut it off."

"Never." She couldn't. Wouldn't.

"Never say never, Red. I won't always be there with a hairbrush."

"I don't need your hairbrush or you brushing my hair, and I won't be cutting my hair," she snapped, tensing right back up. This time she stood, yanked the brush from his hand and finished the brushing in a fury, then practically threw the brush back at him. "And it's none of your business anyway, *Coulson*, what I do, or don't do, with my hair!"

"Care to tell me what that's about?" he asked, clearly taken aback by the fast shift in her mood.

"I'm in a hurry, that's what this is about. I don't have time to sit here and talk about…my hair." With that, she turned and fairly flew off the porch, leaving Adam standing there, wondering what the hell had just happened. One moment they'd been having some nice banter going on between them, then…

He watched her disappear into the night. Watched, wondered, then… "Damn," he muttered, sucking in a sharp breath. "Damn it to hell!" He knew that reaction. Had seen it in a few of his patients…chemotherapy patients, when their hair grew back. The loss of hair was the stigma, a sign of sickness or hopelessness, often dreaded more than the illness itself. When it grew back, in so many of his patients he'd seen a life reborn. Saw the glimmer of hope return, and even blossom. "Son of a…" He swallowed back a hard lump, felt a surge of nausea rising in his gut. She'd had cancer. At some time in her life, Erin had had cancer, and the way he felt about that was indescribable. He shut his eyes for a moment, trying to push back the image, trying to reason with himself that he was totally wrong about this. There could be other things…maybe just a plain old obsession. Or vanity. Maybe…maybe…

There weren't any maybes, though. Not real ones. He was a doctor, and he knew. Knew from experience, knew from his heart because he could feel a band around it right now, squeezing it, trying to break it. Cancer touched other people. Touched his patients. But it had never touched someone he…he was coming to care about.

Cancer. That explained so much.

Turning, Adam crashed through the front door then stood in the entryway in the dark for a moment, trying to make sense of it, taking deep breaths, trying to steady his pulse. Most of all, still willing another explanation to reach up and grab him. But it was no use. The thought of Erin and cancer intertwined in his being as one, burrowing its pernicious way in, not letting go. In response, or protest, or mad-as-hell anger, he threw the hairbrush as hard as he could, threw it at nothing but the darkness, heard it hit the wall and fall to the floor in two pieces. Then he stubbed his toe on one of the two chairs in his cottage and swore at the top of his lungs. Not for the pain shooting up his foot but for…for so many other things he couldn't even define.

Davion glanced over at Erin, who was changing the bandages on Tadeo's hands. "He's been sleeping most of the night. Woke up a couple of times, asked for Adam, then went right back to sleep when he realized he was in the clinic."

"And Pabla hasn't come by to see him yet?"

"She won't," Davion said, too matter-of-factly.

The burns looked better than she'd hoped for. The red wasn't quite so angry, and the blistering not as extensive as she'd expected. All in all, Tadeo was one lucky little boy. Not counting his guardian, though. Erin didn't like her, wouldn't even try pretending that she did. "Why won't she?"

"I mean, she took him in because there was no one else. But she doesn't care about him. Barely takes care of him. And let me tell you, Pabla Reyes is one mean lady, doesn't treat other people nicely either. She worked for my mother for a few days, nearly ran off all the customers she was so rude to them. My mother won't even let her come to Trinique's any more, not for any reason."

"And no one knows why she's this way?"

Davion shrugged. "Some people are difficult just because they want to be. Don't need a reason."

That much was true. Although, admittedly, her father had done a good job of protecting her from the abrasive side of life as much as he could. In her life, she'd rarely encountered disagreeable people like Pabla. "What happened to Tadeo's parents?"

"Don't know for sure. Never asked, never heard anybody say much about it, one way or another. That's the thing about living out here. People take things as they are, don't get themselves bothered with things that don't matter. Tadeo lives with Pabla. She's not good to him, but she doesn't hurt him either. He gets food, he gets clothes…"

"Does he get schooling?"

"He's smart, but I don't know."

"He's a good little boy," she said, while she replaced the gauze on one hand then began to remove the dressing from the other hand. "He deserves…"

"Adam."

She looked over at Davion. "You're right." And Adam needed Tadeo maybe even more than Tadeo needed him. But life wasn't always that simple. People didn't always get together because they needed each other.

"Too bad we don't get to choose those things." Davion

stood ready with fresh gauze, watching intently as Erin went about the second dressing. By now, Tadeo was beginning to rouse.

"Sometimes we do, though," she said. "My father chose me."

"And would you have chosen him?" he asked.

"In a heartbeat."

"No mother?"

No mother, not including those first five years of her life…and even then, her memories of her birth parents were so dim they nearly didn't exist. "No mother." Funny how she couldn't even picture them now. They were faded snapshots, no clear images caught on them any longer.

"I didn't mean to," Tadeo murmured in a groggy haze. "Tell him I'm sorry."

"I know you are," Adam said, stepping up to the bedside. "Accidents happen, and I'm not mad at you."

"But *Stella*," Tadeo cried, as huge tears started sliding his cheeks. "She got burned up. I didn't mean to, and I tried to make the fire stop."

"It's a boat, Tadeo. Boats don't matter. Someday, maybe I can get another boat we can work on together. But right now the important thing here is you. You're what matters, the only thing that matters, and I'm not mad at you."

"And he's doing very nicely," Erin said. "The burns are already beginning to look better."

"But his hands are going to have to stay bandaged for a while," Adam said, "and I doubt Pabla is going to take care of him while he's bandaged. Which means…"

"Which means, the three of us have our work cut out for us," Davion said, backing toward the door. "And with that, I'm going home. Going to sleep for a while, going to study, going to sing and hope for big tips. Let me know when you need me here, and in the meantime I'll check with a few of the ladies in town who might be able to come in and stay with him." He grinned, saluted the lot, then walked away.

"You don't have to be involved with this," Adam said. "I can do it."

"Is this because you don't want me to help? Or is it that you don't need me? Because I'm involved here, Coulson. I've told you that before. Like it or not, I'm part of it. Tadeo's going to need constant care for a while, and even with some of Davion's ladies dropping by, you're going to need more help with Tadeo than you realize."

"And you didn't come to Regina to play…" He glanced down at the boy, who'd drifted back to sleep. "To play nursemaid. It was my boat, my responsibility. I'll take care of things."

What was it with him? One minute he was brushing her hair, the next he was practically hurling her out the door. "You're really a whole sack of mixed messages. Do you know that, Coulson?"

"What I know is that… Why the hell didn't you tell me? Did you think that I wouldn't figure it out eventually?"

"Tell you what? What would you figure out?" Her heart lurched. She knew he knew. But he was a good doctor. Why wouldn't he have guessed it?

"Cancer, Red. You had cancer, didn't you?"

"What makes you think I had cancer?"

"Your hair. You're not an obsessed person, not self-involved at all, but you're overly sensitive about your hair. I've seen it before. Seen how people become so obsessed or overprotective of their hair when it finally grows back. They don't cut it, they don't let people touch it. They run off in near-hysterics when there's a suggestion of cutting."

"So, I have a thing about my hair, and you immediately

jump to the cancer conclusion? And I didn't run off in near-hysterics. I was in a hurry to get to work."

"It wasn't about work, Red," he said gently. "And you did mention a difficult childhood. So, am I wrong about this? *Please*, tell me I'm wrong."

"Is it any of your business if I did have cancer? And I'm not saying that I did. But if I'd had cancer when I was younger, why would you even care?"

"Did you, Red?" His voice was suddenly so soft, so sympathetic, she barely recognized it.

"Why do you need to know? What possible difference would it make about anything?"

He shrugged. "Don't know. I suppose I could say something like I'm curious, and leave it at that. But if things work out for you here, we're in this for the long haul… colleagues. I think that entitles me to…to something."

Colleagues. Well, that just about said everything, didn't it? No point in keeping it to herself because it didn't matter if he knew. Colleagues kept their relationship on a surface level. Nothing deep, nothing involved. Not even a friendship. So there was no point in holding out for anything more. "OK, I had acute lymphocytic leukemia. Primary bout and two recurrences." Now he knew. Let the pushing away begin. Because once people knew, they did start to push away from her. Some did it slowly, trying to be polite. Some just broke into a dead run. For some, though, it was simply the emotional distancing until the separation was so tenuous it simply snapped. However it happened, they always left, except for a very few—her father, Serek and Alvinnia, Mrs Meecham. And Coulson? She honestly didn't know what he'd do. "Totally recovered now. Done with by the time I was fourteen, in case you're interested," she said, drawing herself up defensively on the outside but feeling very wobbly on the inside. One bout of cancer and they were supportive. Two and they became wary. Three and they found it hard to even be in the same room with her. Out of sight, out of mind. That's what she'd always pretended had happened to her parents. They'd simply walked away and forgotten to come back. It made her life simpler that way.

"And that's why the children's hospital is for long-term critical care. It makes sense now."

She wasn't sure where this was going, wasn't sure what to do. Most of all, she wasn't comfortable, and she wanted to get away from him. Go off somewhere by herself for a few minutes and bury those longings he'd been dredging up in her because now, no matter what else happened, they didn't matter. She'd been there before, been the recipient of the same apprehension and uncomfortable feelings. It's the way her life worked. She was used to it, and most of the time it didn't matter. But, then, most of the time she didn't allow herself the feelings she knew she had for Coulson. Because this day always came, and she knew what would happen at the end of it. "Look, I've got to meet an architect in a few minutes. Can you sit with Tadeo for a while?"

He nodded. Didn't say a word. And she left. Didn't look back. Didn't cry. What was the point?

CHAPTER EIGHT

Two days had raced by since the big revelation, and Erin had encountered Coulson coming and going, but that's all. A friendly wave, a quick hello was as far as it went between them except when it came to medical dealings, then they talked about Tadeo or other patients. Nothing more. It was pleasant, but bland. No more little barbs, and she was surprised how much she missed that. But that's how it was going to be with them, and she'd just have to get used to it. Now it was business as usual. They'd settled into their routine.

"You sound tired," Algernon commented. "I'm worried about you, Erin. Are you taking good care of yourself? Getting enough rest? Eating properly?"

Erin switched the phone to her other ear and settled back into her chair. Sighed loudly. She was in her own cottage now. Not quite set up the way she wanted, but it would do. "I'm fine, Dad. Just busy getting the hospital ready. I'm also helping in the clinic here and taking care of a little boy who burned himself." Her dad always worried too much. And he was perceptive. Could hear everything in a sigh or an inflection. "I've got people coming and going at the hospital now, doing renovations, and I'm talking to suppliers, starting to make purchases."

"And that young man…Dr Coulson? Have you two—?"

"Colleagues," she interrupted before he could imply anything. "We've established our medical relationship and I think it will be fine."

"Well, doesn't that just sound clinical."

She knew where he was headed with this, and didn't want to go there. "Because it *is* clinical. That's all it is."

"I talked to Serek the other day. He told me this Dr Coulson had a *look* in his eye for you. He also said that you light up around Dr Coulson. Is there anything to that?"

Ah, yes. Her dear, sweet godfather doing her father's matchmaking bidding. "Uncle Serek is wrong," she said, fighting hard to avoid all inflections so her father would make no more assumptions. "Coulson and I are almost to the place where we can tolerate each other, but that's as far as it goes with us. And you two need to quit trying to pair me off with every man who comes within a mile of me. I'm fine without one, fine doing what I'm doing right now. Oh, and in case you've forgotten, you're not exactly the right person to be matchmaking for me, Mr Confirmed Bachelor. You find yourself a woman first then we'll see what we can do to find me a man. Until that happens, though…"

Algernon laughed. "Now you're sounding like you."

This was the first time she'd heard him laugh in months, and it immediately brought tears to her eyes. Which meant he'd know she was crying, and would probably jump to the wrong conclusions and worry even more. "Look, Dad, I've got to run," she said, fighting back the sniffles. "It's my turn to go sit with Tadeo for a while. He's getting restless, wants to get up and play, and it's taking everything we can do to keep him still."

Algernon didn't comment right away. There was a gap

in the conversation, a long pause, and she knew he was hearing her emotion. All of it. "Look, I'll call you later tonight. OK?" she asked, anxious to end the conversation now.

"He's more than a colleague, isn't he?" he asked. "Answer the question before you hang up, Erin. Is Adam Coulson more than a colleague?"

"No," she whispered. "He is not."

"But you wish…"

"What I wish, Dad, is that you'd quit worrying about me. I'm fine. My health is good, I'm keeping busy. Everything's good."

And it was. Maybe not in her father's definition of the word, but the more she got involved in the life she truly wanted, the better she would be. And Adam Coulson… he was incidental to her plans. She'd fix that in her mind and, sooner or later, it would implant there and make it so. "Where's Tadeo?" she asked Davion ten minutes later.

"Pabla came to get him. Said Tadeo had chores he needed to do, that we couldn't keep him any more."

"Chores? Did you tell her he shouldn't be working? That he can't have his bandages taken off yet, and he still needs bed rest and medication, and absolutely must keep his wounds clean?"

Davion, who was stocking the storeroom shelf with the meager supplies Coulson had brought back with him from Port Wallace, nodded. "I told her everything, but she said to leave them alone. That she doesn't want us butting in any more."

"And Coulson knows this?"

Davion turned around. "Adam went to check on Breeon Edward. Today was her day to come in, but she wasn't up to it so he went to her. So, no, he doesn't know anything about Tadeo yet. Don't expect he'll be too happy about it when he comes back, though."

That was an understatement if ever she'd heard one. Coulson was going to be livid. "Maybe I should go talk to Pabla, tell her how important it is that Tadeo keep his hands bandaged and clean."

"I did. I gave her some clean bandages and she threw them on the floor. She didn't care, Erin. And if I were you, I wouldn't be messing with that lady. She was in a bad mood when she took Tadeo. I told you before, she's mean to the bone."

Mean to the bone maybe. But someone had to look out for Tadeo and since Coulson wasn't here, she felt it had to be her. Felt it in her gut, felt it in her heart. "I can be pretty...mean, too," she said.

Davion laughed at that. "You don't know how to be mean, Erin. You've got a good heart, and right now you're thinking about how you're going to go to Pabla Reyes and convince her to make things good for Tadeo. That somehow a miracle will take place and she'll relate to you in a rational way. Which she will not do. And you're not going to be *mean* about it, even though you know how she's going to act toward you."

"Am I that transparent?" she asked, on a discouraged sigh.

"Yes." He grinned. "That transparent."

Well, that wasn't what she wanted to hear. First her father was reading a whole host of things into what he could hear over the phone, and now Davion was doing the same...reading her like she was a book. An open book. That was the thought that kept running through her head for the next several hours as the carpenters showed up to start building walls in her hospital, and as one of the locals started to install the first of the pickets in the fence Coulson had suggested. She had plumbers on hand, as well as five of the local women who were eager to earn money painting walls. Her hospital was a mass of activity and her presence there was pretty much unnecessary. In fact, she was in the way. And, as it turned out, Davion didn't need her at the clinic as no one was there.

So, since nothing in the hospital's progress needed her supervision, and she wasn't going to go chasing after Pabla, she had time. Time for the beach, she decided on a whim. Why not take a couple of hours and just go and relax? Tell people where she'd be in case anyone needed her. The day was warm, the sky a perfect blue, the water so inviting... why not?

Twenty minutes later, she spread her beach towel in the sand of a fairly secluded little patch of beach. It was hard to imagine, but this was hers. Actually, it belonged to the hospital, but since the hospital was hers...she had a beach! Or a part of one, as the other half still belonged to Coulson.

She pulled off her robe, looked at her conservative black one-piece suit and was overcome with the desire to buy something flowery and skimpy. She wouldn't, of course. But wearing something like that for Coulson, and seeing the expression on his face...

"Not a chance," she quipped, dropping down on her towel. After applying a dab more sunblock to her arms and legs, she lay back and stared up at the sky, trying to empty her mind of everything. No hospital, no worries about her dad or Tadeo. Definitely no Coulson. The harder she tried, though, the more she failed. Especially the part about Coulson. He filled every last nook and cranny, and wouldn't let go. It was aggravating that even in the couple of hours off she was treating herself to, she couldn't truly get away. OK, maybe she wasn't trying hard enough. Maybe it was time to divert her attention, do something other than being idle.

The ocean in front of her took care of that whim. While she wasn't about to go swimming alone, there was no reason why she couldn't go wading. Just splashing about in the surf, wandering in just to her knees… It had been a long time since she'd been to a beach. These past few years her water activities had been limited to taking a shower and an occasional workout in the staff lap pool at the hospital where she'd worked. For her, personal time had always come at a premium. There were too many things to do, too many things to accomplish, and squandering precious time on frivolous endeavors was such a waste. The truth was, she didn't relax very well. Didn't know how. When she'd been young, and hadn't known if she had a future ahead of her, she hadn't been able to relax. Then, when she'd known she was going to have that future, she had been too busy making up for lost time to relax. So it didn't surprise her that as she waded out, and the wet sand oozed between her toes, she felt almost…decadent.

"It's a shallow shoreline here. You can actually go out farther," Coulson called from the path. He'd been watching her for a few moments, not so much to enjoy the very nice view of Erin as much as he was enjoying the way she went about wading, almost the way a child would. And with so much joy. It was like her life was about *firsts*… doing so many things for the first time. Maybe she was. Maybe her past hadn't allowed her the same experiences most people had. He could only imagine how tough it had been…sick for so many years, then going to college and medical school. That was a pretty narrow course, and he doubted she would have ever strayed very far from it. She was too…focused, too determined to accomplish her goals no matter what. Probably the result of so much uncertainty surrounding her leukemia.

But just look at her now! She was beautiful…stunning. The sun catching on glints of her chaotic red hair, her milky-white skin in unsettling contrast to the blue of the ocean waters… Damn, he wanted to fall in love with her. Wanted it badly. And maybe he already had. Another time, another place, he might have been able to act on it. But now it was time to focus on other things. Time to put his own life in order, one way or another. Before Erin, that hadn't seemed to matter so much. He'd got along. Chased that proverbial impossible dream. Avoided…well, avoided everything he could, pretty much. Now, though, it was changing. She was changing him. Her goals were changing him. Which meant it was time he thought about changing himself. He hadn't decided how yet. But change was on the horizon as surely as Erin Glover was the most beautiful thing he'd ever seen on this beach.

Sucking in a sharp breath and squaring his shoulders, Adam headed toward the surf, not sure what he was going to do once he got there. Not sure that the best course right now wouldn't be to turn around and walk away. Not sure about anything.

"If I'm not mistaken, this is a private beach," she said, visoring her eyes with her hand to see him.

Surprisingly, she wasn't making a scramble for her robe the way he'd expected her to. Thank God for small blessings as his eyes were on feast overload and he didn't even care that he was staring openly. "And the sales contract gave me privileges here. Actually, more of a right of way through to my section of private beach." He swallowed hard, deciding it was time to fix his stare somewhere else.

"But you're not dressed for beachcombing."

He looked down at his khaki pants and blue button-down shirt, like he'd momentarily forgotten what he was wearing. "Going down to Port Wallace to catch a shift at the hospital. Had about thirty minutes before I needed to leave, and I thought I'd come to the beach and just relax for a few minutes. I, um…" He deliberately fixed his eyes on a sailboat offshore. Stared at it intently. "I have a little cabana set up on the other side of the cove, and—"

"Davion told you about Pabla taking Tadeo?"

"And I kicked a hole in an appropriate door. You'll see it next time you're in the clinic. The hell of it is, there's nothing I can do about Tadeo except kick that damned hole. Pabla has rights to him, I don't. At this point, I think if we go after him or even approach him, we're going to get ourselves into trouble, which is only going to make more trouble for Tadeo."

"I hate this, Coulson. Hate being so helpless."

He hated it, too. Right now, though, all he could do was wait, worry and hope. And bide his time, because Tadeo *would* find a way back to him. Of that, he was certain. "Pabla will back off after a while. She'll get tired of Tadeo again, and quit watching him so closely. It's happened before."

"I hope so. Because he's at such a critical point in his recovery, and it scares me to think about all the things that can go wrong. So, since we can't fix that situation right now, can I come with you so I can fix someone or something else?" she asked. "Come with you to the hospital, not the cabana."

That snapped him out of his distraction. "What?"

"To the hospital? Can I go with you? I promised Uncle Serek I'd pick up a shift in Emergency whenever I could, and he told me it's an open invitation. So…" She stepped out of the water, brushed by him as she went to retrieve her robe. "Let me give him a call, see if he wants me. You

go relax in your cabana, and if they'll let me have a shift,
I'll be ready to go when you leave."

"You want to work a shift in Emergency on your time
off?"

She smiled. "I miss medicine. I mean, it's great helping
you in the clinic, but I'm third in line after you and Davion,
so I really haven't been of much use. And all this work of
getting the hospital set up…it's necessary. But not what I
enjoy doing."

"You don't ever relax, do you?" Suddenly the luscious
body in the swimsuit was not anywhere near the front of
his thoughts. Even though she hadn't done it in the literal
sense, Erin had figuratively shrouded herself in a white lab
coat. All doctor, all the time. Admirable, but unfortunate.
He doubted she even knew she was so much more than a
doctor or a dutiful daughter.

"Of course I do. What you were standing off the path
watching was me relaxing."

"For how long? Ten minutes?"

She shrugged. "Doesn't matter."

"Sometimes it does," he said, heading away from her.
His wife had been fixed on a lifestyle that had consumed
her. Erin was fixed on work that consumed her. They
weren't the same at all, but in a way they were. So why
the hell was he attracted to the obsessive types when he
hated obsession so much? Would he ever find the woman
who knew how to strike the balance he wanted? Because
more than anything else, he needed balance in his life. He
desperately needed balance. "See you in thirty," he called
over his shoulder, without looking back.

"Why here?" she asked, after twenty *long*, silent minutes when the only sound came from the tires on the
rutted road.

"What?"

"Jamaica. The less-traveled places. Why did you choose this as where you wanted to practice medicine?"

"Didn't," he said. "It chose me. I had an opportunity to come out with some mission doctors, sort of an offset to some of my medical tuition, and I found…home. I liked it. It fit me, I fit it. Decided to stay."

"And your wife didn't agree with the decision?" That was probably overstepping the boundary, but she was curious. And even if they couldn't be involved as anything other than friends or colleagues, friends and colleagues did have some intrusion privileges. So she was intruding a bit. "She wasn't the island paradise sort?"

He visibly winced over that one. "I thought she was. Stupid me, I forgot to ask. So you can imagine how surprised I was when, after a year or so into our marriage, I opened my eyes to find out she was on the corporate track. She wanted to be an administrator, not a doctor who gave patient care. She wanted position and prestige and I wanted…Jamaica."

"That's a big difference?"

"Especially when you embarrass your wife."

"What did you do to embarrass her?"

"I was me. I worked in a free clinic, came to Jamaica to give free care whenever I could. Used our marital assets to do it and didn't include her on that decision because I knew what she'd say. One day she told me that I loved the kind of medicine I practiced more than I loved her. And I accused her of the same thing, loving her career more than she loved me. As it turned out, we were both so right, we couldn't argue it. So, where do you go from there, except to a divorce lawyer? The thing is, in that divorce, they gave her everything but my grandfather's inheritance and *Stella*, because the judge figured I'd already spent my fair share of our assets on my various medical pursuits. Which is probably the case. So…that's it, the story of my pathetic life."

"Not pathetic. Admirable, Coulson. It's unfortunate that your marriage didn't survive, but there's nothing pathetic about your choices or the way you live your life."

"Well, whatever way you want to look at it, she's fine, I'm fine. And we're both right where we want to be, so it's not all bad."

"Most people never get to live the dream. Yours may not be turning out exactly the way you'd planned it, but you're living it. So rather than saying it's not all bad, I think you should say it's pretty much all good."

"Ah, yes. The optimist."

"Someone has to be," she said.

"So, now that you know all my secrets, tell me some of yours. Like why you've never made a commitment to anybody. Not in the for ever-after or marriage kind of sense. Or maybe you did, and it didn't work out."

"Maybe because the person I am knows the foibles I have. You said it yourself, that I never relax. Earlier, at the beach, ten minutes of playtime and I was ready to go. You saw that. And look! Here I am now, getting ready to work again. It's what I do. Who I am. All I am, and nothing about that would make it easy for someone else to find their way in."

"Don't underestimate yourself. I have an idea if you take a good, hard look at yourself, you're going to see a woman who wouldn't let anything she wants stand in her way, work or otherwise. And there's a whole lot of *otherwise* in you, Red. You're just not ready to see it yet. Or maybe you're too stubborn to see it. But it's there, when you decide to look."

"Is that a compliment?" she asked. It was nice being

perceived as substantial when so much of her life she'd been thought of as weak or languishing. But Coulson had never seen her during those days and he was basing his impression on what he saw now. It pleased her, actually. "It could be."

"Well, then, I think I'll take it as a compliment." A compliment with lingering good feelings that lasted all the rest of the way to the hospital and on through the first few patients she saw.

"You doing OK?" Coulson asked, on a fast pass through the corridor on his way to have a look at a broken leg.

"Busy. Nothing complicated."

"Well, I have complicated for you. Down in the first exam room. She wants to see you, insists on it, won't let me anywhere near her. She said she knew there was a lady doctor working tonight, and—"

"I'll get it," Erin said, snapping off her pair of gloves and grabbing a fresh pair from the box on the shelf next to the sink. So far, she'd treated abrasions, stomach aches, headaches, menstrual cramps…not a bad night. But she was ready for a challenge. And as it turned out, her complicated patient was just that. Complicated. She was a tiny, old lady, somewhere north of seventy, Erin guessed. Flawless ebony skin, pure white hair, sharp brown eyes. Arms folded tight across her chest. Very precise about what she wanted.

"I won't take my clothes off, young lady. That's not fitting." She was dressed well, in a nice flowered dress of red and yellow, white gloves, dressy hat, enormous red beads to match her bright red lipstick.

"But to examine you—"

"You'll listen to my symptoms, that's how you'll examine me." Miss Francelle Henry proceeded to pull a list from her black patent-leather purse…one that matched her black patent leather shoes. "Then we'll discuss how you will proceed to treat me."

"Yes, ma'am," Erin said, impressed with the woman. "But you've got to understand, Miss Henry, that in order to treat you, I may have to examine you. We'll discuss it first, though, to see what's appropriate."

Miss Henry mulled it over for a moment then nodded. "As long as you don't treat me like that other doctor who came in here and insisted, right off, that I open my dress so he could listen to my heart. Brash young man." She shook her head in clear disapproval. "Rough manners."

Erin could see Coulson as brash. But rough manners? That brought a smile to her face, because she liked the roughness. It was tempered with an odd gentleness that came out in the strangest ways and places, however. Part of his charm, which, it seemed, had escaped Miss Henry. "So, please tell me your symptoms."

She cleared her throat, as if preparing to recite. "Feeling tired and sleeping more than usual. Feeling the cold more than normal. Dry skin, thinning hair. Brittle nails. Sore muscles. Slow movements. General weakness. A hoarse or croaky voice. A change in my facial expression. Depression. Problems with my memory and concentration. Weight gain. Fertility problems. Slowed heart rate."

Fertility problems? That brought a smile to Erin's face. "Are you currently receiving treatment for any of these symptoms, Miss Henry?"

"I've been here three times, and every time I have, that young man has been the one to see me, and he refuses to give me any medication."

"Would you excuse me while I step out of the room for a moment and ask him about it?"

"You tell him for me that I'm having a real doctor take care of me now."

"I will, Miss Henry," she promised.

Coulson was waiting for her in the hall. Smiling. "Diagnosis?"

"She's either got a fairly good medical textbook or access to the internet. So what am I supposed to do with a woman her age who's making up symptoms? In my pediatric practice, I tell them why doing that is a bad thing and tell their parents."

"She's alone, never married. Needs attention. This is the best she gets, I suppose."

"But she's healthy?"

"As the proverbial horse. Although she won't let me touch her. I think she's afraid I'll discover her little scam."

Erin swatted him on the arm. "It's not a scam. Like you said, she just needs attention."

"She and her sister spent a lifetime together, but her sister died a few months ago, and Miss Henry comes here now because there are people around."

It didn't take but a split second for an idea to form.

"Didn't you say the bus from Regina comes here three times a week?"

"What are you thinking of doing, Red? I recognize that devious glint in your eye."

"I'm trying to figure out a way Miss Henry can have her attention. Is she good for the bus ride, you think?"

"What I think is that you're cute as hell when you're being devious."

"No wonder she says you're brash!"

Back in the exam room, Erin convinced Miss Henry that she had to give her an exam. As it turned out, her blood pressure was perfect, so was her heart rate. Her reflexes were amazing for a woman her age, and her eyesight was perfect without glasses. "What I think, Miss Henry, is that your symptoms will disappear once you pick up your activity level. You've become too sedentary."

"No pills?"

Erin shook her head. "Pills would only slow you down."

"Then tell me, young lady, how I'm supposed to pick up my activity level. I take a walk every day. I clean my house, cook for myself."

"Get a job," Erin said in all seriousness.

"You're as brash as that young man. You know that no one will hire someone my age to work. Besides that, good jobs are scarce in Port Wallace, and I'll not take anything other than a *good* job."

"I would hire you. And the job I'm offering is better than anything you could hope to find here."

Miss Henry's face registered total surprise. "What kind of job?" she asked suspiciously.

"As a nursing assistant. I'm opening up a hospital in Regina for critically ill children who need long-term care. As a nursing assistant, you would read to them, help them with activities such as dressing, bathing, eating. Push them in wheelchairs if necessary, accompany them on short walks. Play games. Maybe even do some teaching since we'll have to maintain their schoolwork. It's all very important work, Miss Henry, and while I know it's a long bus ride for you, too long to go back and forth every day, what I thought we might do is have you come to Regina and stay in one of the guest cottages for a day or two each week, then return to your home for a few days. Would you be interested?"

"I'd have to think about it," she said, trying to sound matter-of-fact, when the expression in her eyes revealed so much more.

It was all Erin could do to hold back tears. In a way,

it was like the day her father had first discovered her. At the time, she hadn't known there was such a long journey ahead, but there had been. And there was for Miss Henry, too, and Miss Henry had just realized it. "You can let me know. Leave a message for me here as soon as you've decided, then we'll work out the details." She was sure Leron Edward would be more than happy to help with the transportation since one of the things Breeon had mentioned to her was that they'd like to find a way to pay for their medical services. A bus ride every few days would do nicely.

"You do think this will cure my symptoms?" she asked, heading toward the door.

"Miss Henry, I can guarantee that once you keep yourself busier, you'll feel much better."

With a curt nod, Francelle Henry exited the exam room, dropping the list of her complaints in the trash can on her way out.

"Well?" Coulson asked, poking his head in the door a moment later.

"List in the trash, and I have a new nursing assistant. It's been a very good evening."

"You're a miracle worker, Red. Miss Henry has been looking for her cure for months, and no one's been able to figure it out."

Maybe the ones who tried didn't know what it was like to be left behind. Age didn't matter, because emptiness was emptiness, and it was a terrible feeling. Shortly, Miss Henry would have something to fill that emptiness and Erin would have herself one sparky old lady who would be a tremendous asset to the hospital. Miracle, no. But very good.

CHAPTER NINE

"TADEO'S running a fever," Davion shouted through her front door. "Erin, can you hear me? It's Tadeo."

She hadn't been asleep more than an hour. Her shift and a half in the emergency room had gone by surprisingly fast, and she'd loved it. There hadn't been any real emergencies, but the pace of everyday treatment had stayed consistent for the twelve hours she'd worked, and by the time they'd made the long drive home and she'd crawled into bed, she'd been able to feel it…in her legs, in her lower back, in her shoulders.

"Erin, wake up!"

This time she did, realizing that Davion had an emergency. Pulling on her robe, she flew to the front door.

"He's burning up. Delirious. I think Pabla must have left him on the steps because when I went over to the clinic to open up this morning, he was there."

"Where's Coulson?"

"Off to check on Breeon Edward again. She had a rough night. May be in labor."

"Give me two minutes to dress, and I'll be right there." Two minutes were actually only one, and Erin was running out the door and across the compound as hard and as fast as she'd ever run. Her hair wasn't combed, she was wearing last night's clothes, and none of it mattered. *Tadeo was sick*. Twenty-four hours with Pabla and he was sick.

"Erin?" A voice called to her from across the compound.

She stopped. Spun round. "Dad?" There he was, suitcase in hand, with Mrs Meecham, who was also holding a suitcase.

"I was worried. You didn't sound right, so I decided we'd better come and see what was going on. See if there was some way I could help you."

Her dad had always come through for her, and her heart swelled with love just seeing him here. But she didn't have time for him right now. "Look, Dad, I have an emergency. A very sick little boy…I can't stop now. Sorry…" With that, she continued her run to the clinic, where she found Tadeo in the first exam room. Davion was removing the bandages from his hands, and even from the door she could smell the vile stench of infection. It had spread so quickly, and she couldn't even begin to imagine what Pabla had forced him to do to cause that. Her heart immediately clutched, thinking of all the ways this could have happened.

"Skin's gone purple," Davion said. "More swelling, green discharge."

"Probably pseudomonas," Erin said, running to the shelf to find a pair of gloves.

"In this area, I would suspect *P. mallei*, or *Burkholderia mallei*, as it's more commonly called. Possibly glanders, too, if he's come into contact with contaminated soil, water or anything else a sick horse or mule might have touched." Algernon stepped into the room and, like his daughter, donned a pair of exam gloves. "I think we're looking at two separate conditions…the infection as the primary problem, with glanders as the result."

"Glanders," she murmured. Glanders could cause lung

damage, exacerbate cardiac problems, and it was marked by coughing, fever, runny nose, swollen eyes. Death was possible, and in her opinion Tadeo was nearing death. "I know what the textbooks say on how to treat it, but I've never seen it," she said to her dad.

"Not in Chicago, you wouldn't have. It's pretty well limited to certain places in the world now, and then only to the more rural areas. Like this."

"So it would have entered Tadeo through his burns?"

"And spread. Like wildfire, as they say. The incubation period can be very short, hours maybe, especially if the person infected has another underlying problem."

Her dad was still so vital, it made her proud. Now all she had to do was convince him that he was badly needed. Maybe this was a start because he was in charge here, the way he should be. No one would ever dispute that. "He also has a heart murmur."

"Untreated, I'm assuming. Probably no diagnosis of the problem and I'm speculating we don't know to what degree he's compromised, if at all. And I'd be willing to wager that he hasn't had a tetanus shot either."

The thought of that caused her to cringe. "He's been medically neglected. His guardian won't allow medical care, and we haven't been able to convince her."

"But he's here now, so we start the process with him in order to get him well again."

Spoken with no indecision. It felt so right, having her father back this way. This was, indeed, where he belonged. "Did you hear that, Tadeo? That's my father, the best doctor in the whole wide world, and he's going to make you better."

"He wouldn't have to if Tadeo being sick hadn't been such an inconvenience to Pabla in the first place," Davion snapped. "But I'm betting that she won't want anything to do with him now that he's in this condition."

Algernon looked at Erin and smiled. "Then it's a good thing she gave him to those who want him, isn't it?"

Swallowing back the lump in her throat, Erin turned to Davion as he finished plucking the remaining sheds of bandages from Tadeo's hands. "He needs oxygen," she said, and in an instant Davion was out the door on his way to get an oxygen tank.

"He's also going to need a hospital," Algernon said. He handed over her stethoscope, the one with her initials engraved on it, the one he'd given her the day she'd graduated from college. "Thought you might like a few of your medical tools."

She took a quick listen to Tadeo's chest. It was gurgly with fluid, his heartbeat irregular. Tadeo was dying and there was nothing here that could save him. "The hospital is two hours away, and I don't think he has much more than two hours in him," she said.

"Who?" Coulson asked, joining the group in the tiny exam room. He looked down at the exam table, and all the color drained from his face. "Damn," he muttered, grabbing the wall for support.

Erin went immediately to his side, pushed him gently back into the hall. "He's infected. Badly. My father thinks it might be glanders…"

"Your father?" he asked, suddenly noticing the older man also standing in the tiny group.

"Tadeo's heart is compromised, Coulson. He's having difficulty breathing. Davion's putting oxygen on him right now, and he's not responsive. We've got to get him to the hospital or—"

"Breeon's in labor," he said. "I brought her in with me because it's going to be soon. Baby hasn't turned yet, but

I think it's going to happen. She said you stopped by the other day, gave her some exercises to do?"

Erin shrugged. "Sometimes it works. Anyway, one of us has to go, the other has to stay."

"I'll stay," Algernon volunteered, stepping into the conversation. "I'll keep that young man, Davion, with me, and Glenda as well."

"Glenda?" Coulson asked.

"Mrs Meecham," Erin explained. "She's a social worker and an old family friend. She's moving here to work at the hospital with us."

"The three of us will be able to deliver the baby," Algernon said. "While the two of you tend to the boy."

"But, Dad, it might be breech," Erin protested.

"And how many breech babies have you delivered, young lady?" he asked.

"None."

"I've delivered dozens. So go. You and Dr Coulson go and take care of that boy because he'll be needing both of you. We'll take care of things here while you're gone."

Coulson looked at her, as if to ask whether Algernon was still fit to work, and she gave him a barely perceptible nod. This was Algernon Glover after all. The most amazing doctor she'd ever known. A lump formed in her throat just thinking about her dad working as a doctor once more. "We will," she whispered, finally giving her dad the long-overdue hug.

"And, Dr Coulson," Algernon said, while Erin was still clinging to him, "you tell Serek that you need supplies here. Tell him to give you what's required and send the bill to me. I know that budgets are tight and medical supplies not in abundant quantity here, but I expect that if my old friend looks hard enough, maybe calls in a few favors, he'll be able to do something for you. If I'm going to be pressed into service here from time to time, which it seems I will be, I'll need better than what you have to offer. Do you hear me, young man?"

"Yes, sir," Coulson said, sounding almost intimidated.

"Isn't he something?" Erin said, on her way over to the next room to have a quick chat with Breeon while Coulson readied Tadeo for transport.

"Well, I see where you get it. Like father, like daughter."

"You think so?" she said, beaming.

"I think so."

"If that isn't just about the nicest thing anybody's ever said to me." Impulsively, she stood on tiptoe and kissed him on the cheek. "Don't worry, my dad will take good care of Breeon," she whispered in his ear.

Mrs Meecham had found her way into Breeon's room and was holding her hand when Erin came in. "Your timing's not very good," she said to Breeon as she gave her old friend a hug.

"I heard the little boy is very ill," Mrs Meecham said.

"We have to take him to the hospital in Port Wallace. Dad's going to stay here and look after Breeon."

"I'll be fine," Breeon said. "Pains aren't too bad yet. Maybe Davion could stay and help me if I need it before you come back."

"He will, but, like I said, my father is going to be here, too. And he'll deliver your baby if we don't get back in time."

"Has your father done this before?" Breeon asked, her face marked with concern.

"My father is a doctor in the United States. In my opinion, the best doctor in the world. He's delivered more babies than most doctors, and if your baby stays breech, he can take care of that, too."

"Will you stay, too?" Breeon asked Mrs Meecham. The bond between the women was already forming.

"I'd love to stay. And what she says about Algernon is true. There's no finer doctor anywhere."

"Algernon?" Breeon asked. "Your name is Glover, Erin, so would your father be *the* Algernon Glover?"

Erin nodded.

"It's a miracle!" Breeon cried, breaking into an ear-to-ear grin. "Meant to be. He's the doctor who delivered me. My parents were from Alligator Pond, and he was there once, visiting…"

"My grandmother," Erin supplied.

"Your grandmother?"

Erin nodded. "Odessia Glover."

"My mother worked for Miss Odessia, in her office. She went into labor and your father was there. He delivered me in that very office. And now he will deliver my baby." Tears rolled down Breeon's cheeks. "It's a miracle that brought you here…all of you. Everything will be fine with me and my baby. Now, go and take care of the little boy."

Five minutes later, Coulson sat in the backseat of his car holding Tadeo, while Erin drove. Neither of them spoke for a while. Mostly, she concentrated on the road while he concentrated on taking Tadeo's vital signs and wiping down the boy's head with cool, wet rags Davion had sent along.

"He's not going back there," Coulson finally said. "When we pull him through this, Pabla's not getting him back. And I don't care who I have to fight over this." He meant it. He didn't care what he had to do, he was never going to let Tadeo go and live with that woman again.

"Davion doesn't think she'll want him back," she said, swerving to avoid a bump. "He doesn't have much of an opinion of Pabla anyway, and he's pretty sure she'd done with Tadeo now. That's why she brought him to you."

"Well, let's hope he's right, because I'd rather do this the easy way than have to fight her over it."

"You mean, adopt him?"

He hadn't thought that far. But, to tell the truth, it sounded right. Him, a father. He glanced down at Tadeo, and his gut churned. A would-be father with one very sick little boy. A little boy who, even after he was over the crisis, would take a long time to completely heal. Yet, in spite of it all, he would adopt him if that option came his way. "Yes, if the magistrate here will grant that."

"Even though you know how sick he's going to be for a while? And that his recovery could take months, maybe longer?"

"Eyes wide open." He picked up his stethoscope and listened to Tadeo's chest again.

As Erin glanced back over the seat, that's when she knew she loved Coulson. Oh, there had been hints, she'd been on the verge of admitting it to herself. But right now, at nine-nineteen in the morning, on a Tuesday, that's when she knew she did love him with all her heart, when she knew there was no turning back. And the bonus that came with Coulson was Tadeo. In her wildest imaginings she could picture them all as a family, which was odd, because she'd never before considered herself as part of anything other than what she was already a part of. Where she was now, it was safe, and she loved safety. But stepping outside that protective little net? It scared her, especially as Coulson hadn't so much as cast her an interested glance.

Didn't matter, though. Not right now, anyway. Her feelings were involved and it was going to take some time for her to get used to them. So it was just as well that he wasn't involved in this because, she suspected, she wouldn't do it very well anyway.

Still, she did love him.

"Not good," Coulson said, slumping down in the chair in the doctors' lounge. It was a small, gray room affording doctors only a place to get away from the masses of humanity lining the halls. No luxuries but a coffee pot. Coffee wasn't always available, but that was fine because, right now, his stomach was already filled with bitter acid. He didn't need any more to add to it. "They're going to have to surgically debride his hands, and treating him for the glanders goes without saying. But they're not sure what's going to kick it because he's septic." Meaning the infection had spread through his bloodstream.

"No," she gasped. "It happened so fast."

"And it only gets worse from there."

She hated asking because she already knew. But the words had to be said aloud because doing so made it a very real problem to deal with, not just one put off in the background somewhere. And Tadeo had a very real problem. "His heart?"

He looked over at her, his eyes answering every question she could possibly ask. The two of them were sitting directly across from each other, their knees practically touching, and she could feel the tension in him even from there. The pressure of it all, the stress, the overwhelming gravity of Tadeo's condition was so dense in that little room it was nearly sucking out all the oxygen. She could feel it in her lungs, in the way they were fighting her. Coulson felt it too, in that impenetrable blanket of dread slipping down over him. It was there, in the way he moved, the way he sat in the chair, the way he breathed.

"His heart," he confirmed. "ASD. Tests are conclusive."

ASD, or atrial septal defect, was a deformity in the septum between the heart's two upper chambers—the septum being the wall separating the heart's left and right sides. Septal defects were commonly referred to as holes in the heart.

"Small, large?"

"The defect itself is on the smaller side, and that's probably the best news I've got right now. It can be corrected by surgery, with a fairly good rate of total recovery, but only after they get all the other problems cleared up in him first. And right now they're afraid the infection could spread to his heart, which could mean…" He stopped, looked up at the ceiling. "Right now, the biggest problem is curing the infection and preventing it from doing any more damage than it may have already done. Besides that, they have to get him into surgery for the burns because if they don't he could lose his hands, but the damn surgery is a huge risk in itself, because he's so sick, and it's never good to operate on someone with the kind of systemic infection Tadeo has. So…" He shrugged. "It's not good, Red. Not good any way they do it."

Erin leaned forward, placed her hand on his knee. "Then we'll take it one step at a time, and work with whatever comes up whenever we need to. That's really the only way you can deal with a critical illness because if you think too far into the future, or plan on too many things, you could lose focus on the one single thing you should be concentrating on right now…which is getting Tadeo the surgery he needs for his hands. And I know that sounds pretty frustrating, especially when you'd like to jump right in and fix everything at once, but we both know that can't happen. So for now we'll do whatever the doctors think is necessary, and do whatever we have to minute by minute, if that's what it takes. Trust the doctors, too, because they will take good care of him, Coulson. Uncle Serek's overseeing his case, and I trust him with Tadeo the way my father trusted him with me. The way I trust you, too."

"You're including me in some pretty fine medical company, Red."

"Because you deserve to be included there."

He didn't reply to that. But he sighed heavily, probably finding it difficult to focus on anything but Tadeo. It was tough, being the parent of a critically sick child. She'd worked with those parents. More than that, she'd seen how it had affected her father, and what she'd seen in him was what she was now seeing in Coulson. Being a doctor made it worse, too, because you knew more, even though you couldn't do more. Or, in this case, couldn't do anything but be one of those forced to sit and wait, and pray for good news. "Don't forget that Tadeo's a tough little boy. He can fight the odds, and he will once he knows that he has people who love him fighting for him...*you* fighting for him."

"It's crazy, how one thing can set off a whole chain of events, isn't it? I was teaching him how to work on the boat, do some woodwork, maybe help him with a skill that would come in handy later in his life, and now he's on the verge of dying because of it." He shut his eyes, leaned his head back against the wall. "Who the hell am I kidding, Red? I don't have a damn thing to offer the people in Regina. Medical care on a shoestring doesn't work, and that's all I've got...a shoestring."

"And a dream," she said.

"Yeah, well...dreams *don't* come true, do they? I'm the living proof of that!"

She withdrew her hand from his knee. "The thing is, Coulson, you're wrong. Dreams can come true, but sometimes you have to work for your dream in ways you'd never expected to."

"You think I haven't been working? What the hell gives you the right to say that? Because all I do is work. And look how it turns out. Tadeo may die because of me…"

"Because of you?"

"Because I am a dreamer. I know I am. My first wife accused me of it, told me I didn't have any idea how to be practical. But stupid me, I thought coming to a place that needed medical care as badly as Regina does *was* a practical plan. You know, operate a nice little clinic, open up a small hospital, get my boat restored. Perfect plan, perfect life. Turns out I was wrong all the way round because I don't have any of that, do I?"

"So, what are you going to do? Quit? Turn your back on everything you've started here and walk away? Wish Tadeo better luck with his next guardian, tell Davion he's going to have to find another way to get himself to medical school because his *scholarship* has decided to drop out, then go and start a different life in a place without complications?"

"Sounds a hell of a lot better than the life I've started here."

"You know you don't mean that. You love that little boy like he's your own son, and right now he needs you to be his dad. As far as Davion's concerned, he'll save lives, be a great doctor who will make a difference in this world. He's got heart and instinct for it like few people have, and you know it. You want to be part of it—why else would you be saving every penny you make, working every day and every night, just to get him into medical school?"

"You know about that?"

"Davion knows about that, Coulson. You're not exactly good at keeping your secrets." She smiled. "He wants you to be proud of him, the way Tadeo does. And that's impact, like it or not. You're important to these boys and they're important to you, and you don't have the heart to walk away. Deep down, you don't even have that secret desire because you're a true humanitarian. I came here thinking I was, and I was also being pretty pretentious about it. But there you were, doing the good things in quiet ways."

"Not pretentious. Just stubborn."

"That, too." Glancing up at the clock on the wall, she sighed. The wait was so long, so agonizing. She'd never been on this end of it before. She'd been the patient, the doctor, but never the one who was supposed to sit and wait patiently, and she wasn't doing a very good job of it. In fact, she was about ready to jump out of her skin. "You know, I need to get out of here for a few minutes."

"Want to go for a walk?"

"You don't have to go with me."

"Maybe I need to. I don't do this very well either."

"You were reading my mind?" she asked.

"Didn't have to. Everything shows on your face."

Erin stared at him. Now Coulson was telling her she wasn't as good at hiding her emotions as she'd believed, and she didn't know what to think about that. Didn't have time to think about it, actually, because as she stood to leave the cramped room, the ominous call of Code Blue burst over the loudspeaker system. Adam and Erin responded instinctively, running out the lounge door and heading to…

"No," Erin choked, stopping abruptly in the hall when she realized where the other medical personnel were heading. It was to Tadeo's room. She couldn't let Coulson be there, couldn't let him see… "You can't go down there," she said, spinning around and physically shoving her palm into his chest to stop him.

"He needs me," Coulson said, trying to push past her. But she stepped in front of him, three times to be exact. Planted her full body weight down as an obstacle and shoved him back. But he kept coming right back at her, trying to get through.

"You can't do this." This time she shoved him back with both her hands. "Coulson, you can't go in there! Do you hear me? You can't go into that room and if you try, I'll have the security guard remove you."

This time he stopped. Then he simply stood in the middle of the hall, looking like he didn't know what to do. "Maybe it's not Tadeo," he finally whispered.

"It's Tadeo," she said as steadily as she could, even though all she wanted to do was cry. But for Coulson, and for Tadeo, she had to be strong. "They wouldn't put another patient in a burn room due to the high infection risk."

"They could have transferred him…"

"It's Tadeo," she said again, as much for her own benefit as his.

"How could this be happening?" he asked, his voice so deep in anguish it was barely recognizable. He backed up to the wall, slumped against it, and shut his eyes. Waiting. Forcing himself to breathe. "How could so many things be going wrong?"

Honestly, she didn't know. She'd seen that downward spiraling in some of her own patients…that chain of events where one unfortunate circumstance triggered an avalanche. But to see it happening to someone personal to her…Dear God, the pain was unbearable, and the fear overwhelming. She loved that little boy. Not because she loved Coulson and Coulson loved him, but because he'd found a place in her heart she hadn't even known existed. More than that, she identified with him. He was the abandoned child, the one tossed out, the one who was dying. She'd been that child, too. Been the one just left on that figurative doorstep to die if no one took care of her, or live if they did. Like Tadeo.

"It happened because some people are miserable excuses

for human beings," she said, surprised by the venom in her words. "They're selfish. Heartless. Contemptible."

Coulson opened his eyes, startled by the raw anger in her words. He'd seen her through a number of different emotions, but never this. "Are you OK, Red?" he said.

She shook her head. "No, I'm not. I'm so angry I don't know what to do. Pabla…she's to blame. She threw him away when she could no longer ignore his physical condition. Dropped him off in a nursing home, a place with no children. A place children shouldn't ever have to live, or even know exists. But she didn't care about that. It was a medical facility, it assuaged her guilt, and she went on her merry way. They both did. Lied to me, then left me there to die!" She swiped back an angry tear. "They knew I didn't belong there, in that awful place, but they just…" She looked up at him through a haze of tears.

"They didn't care, Coulson. All they wanted was to get rid of me, and they didn't even say goodbye. They just walked away. Said they'd see me tomorrow, and walked away. And I waited, Coulson. For days, for weeks… Sometimes at night I'd think I hear them sneaking into my room to kiss me goodnight, but it was always a night nurse, making sure I was tucked in or bringing me medicine." She swallowed hard. "You're not supposed to put children in places like that. The nurses there took good care of me because no one knew what to do with me and Mrs Meecham wanted to find someplace else for me, maybe a foster home. But no one wants to take in a child with leukemia. And the courts decided that because I was already getting good enough care, I had to stay in the nursing home until other arrangements could be made. But the thing is, there were no other arrangements. That was it for me. I had a roof, three meals, my medicine, and that was good enough. Until my dad found me. Until you found Tadeo."

Without a word, Adam stepped forward and pulled Erin into his arms. "He's going to have a lot to overcome when he's better, isn't he?" he said. "Emotionally, as well as physically."

"He will get better. He has to. And I'm sorry," she said, not willing to step away from him. His arms felt good around her. She needed to be here, just like this, with him holding her, and her holding him. Because, deep down, they both knew what could happen with Tadeo in the next minutes. Or hours, if he got past the minutes. Or days, if he got past the hours. "I made this about me, and it's not. I shouldn't have done that."

"But it is about you, because you care for him, and you understand him in ways no one else can." Adam tightened his embrace on Erin as Serek Harrison stepped into the hall, his face wearing as grim an expression as Adam had ever seen on a doctor.

He wasn't ready for this. Couldn't be ready for this. All he could do was hold on to Erin and hope…

"I'll be honest with you," Serek started out. He laid a hand on Adam's shoulder. "I didn't think we were going to pull him through it, but we did."

"He didn't…" Erin started, but couldn't bring herself to say the word.

"He's not in good shape. Not at all. But he's still with us, fighting to stay with us as hard as his little body will let him fight."

Finally, Adam let out the breath he'd been holding for what seemed like for ever. "So what happened?"

"He's weak, the septicemia got to his heart. As his heart was already weakened from his untreated murmur, it just gave out. But…he's in normal sinus rhythm now. Breathing on a ventilator but holding his own as best he can. And that's about all I can tell you at this point. We're going to get him into the operating room in just a few minutes and get his hands cleaned up, because until we get at the source of the infection, it's only going to get worse. Given his current condition, I don't have to tell you how risky that's going to be. But we've got to start somewhere with him, because his heart surgery isn't going to be put off too long. Unfortunately, I think we're going to have to take a huge risk in a number of different ways, and do it all within the next day or two…the first round of surgeries and treatments of what I think will be several rounds. And I hate like hell opening him up when he's so infected, but the only thing I can promise you at this point is that if we don't, he's not going to survive another crisis."

"His guardian abandoned him, so what kind of permissions do you need?"

Serek shook his head. "We've already taken care of that. For now, he's in the custody of the hospital. The magistrate's concern was for the child first. But, Adam, since you seem to be close to the boy, we do want you to be in on the decisions we're going to be making."

He would do that, of course. But he wasn't sure he was steady enough at this point. It was for Tadeo, though. Anything to get Tadeo through this. "Whatever you say," he said.

"I say let's get Dr Freeman notified that the surgery is a go. He's the best we've got, and that little boy of yours deserves the best."

"Just like I got the best," Erin said, pushing away from Coulson's chest to give Serek a kiss on the cheek. "Thank you," she whispered. "You know how much I love you, don't you, Uncle Serek?"

"Oh, I know. But I think there are other people who might be needing some of that, too. And one more thing. I talked to Algernon not five minutes ago."

"Breeon?" Coulson asked.

"Doing well. Baby wasn't breech. Healthy little boy, named…" he shook his head and smiled "…Algernon Adam Edward. Now, if that isn't one big mouthful. Mother is fine, baby is fine and the doctor is sounding better than I've heard him sound in months."

Erin heaved a sigh of relief. Then fell back into Coulson's arms, a place she wanted to stay.

CHAPTER TEN

"So, What happens now?" she asked, collapsing on a towel in the sand and looking up at Coulson, who was ankle-deep in the surf, just standing there, gazing out over the water. Throughout the course of the past seven days, they'd been back and forth to the hospital to see Tadeo, never together, though, since one of them needed to tend the clinic. Her dad had fallen into the routine of part-time doctor quite nicely, too, and it was amazing to Erin how many people came just to see the legendary Dr Algernon Glover. He was a local hero here, and it made her proud, seeing her dad in that position. It was good to watch him in action again. Davion was his eyes for the things he could no longer discern. So was Mrs Meecham. All of it a simple solution that warmed her heart in a way she'd lost for a while.

Oh, her father would still continue on his road to total blindness. There was nothing to prevent that from happening. But she had an idea that even in his darkness he would find his own light. A new one, where he felt useful again. Because he was, after all, Algernon Glover. And Algernon Glover had come home into his element, the way his daughter had, at last, found hers. This was her Jamaica now, she was no longer the tourist, and she understood why Coulson could have never given it up. Every bit of life she could ever want for herself was here.

"Who knows what's going to happen?" Coulson answered half-heartedly. "I suppose it's all up to the magistrate. Pabla's gone. Picked up and moved away. No one knows where and the authorities don't seem to care, given the circumstances. Their concern is for the child, so I'm pretty sure they'll let me keep Tadeo since he's going to need so much medical care for a while."

"And more heart surgery," she added. "I think he may be my first patient when we finally open the hospital doors." She and Coulson hadn't talked much about the progression of things to come these past days. No time. Possibly too many emotions spent over the course. But the hospital details were coming together. Her father and Mrs Meecham were seeing to the things she should have been but didn't have time for. As it stood, they anticipated opening its doors in a couple of weeks, and she'd already had contacts from various medical facilities inquiring into the possibility of sending children her way. The need was becoming more and more clear and she could already see the promise of expansion in the future.

"Actually, I was thinking about taking him to a rehab center in the States. There's one in Cleveland that does amazing things for children with cardiac problems. And a friend of mine near there has an opening in his medical practice, so…" he shrugged "…I'm thinking, what the hell? Maybe it's time to change my life again."

"What?" she choked out, totally shocked by that. He wanted to leave? She couldn't believe that. How could he, after he'd given up so much to be here? "Why? This was… everything for you. Everything you ever wanted."

He shrugged. Didn't turn to look at her directly. "A lot of dreams. Very little practicality. As it out turns out, I'm not a very practical man so maybe it's time for me to quit dreaming and commit to some of that practicality. You know, find a focus. I mean, look at me. I'm thirty-six years old, divorced. I work in a bar, moonlight in an E.R., travel from town to town with a medical bag I can't even afford to stock. I practice medicine on the run, didn't have a damn stethoscope until you gave me one, and had this dream that a simple practice and an old restored boat were all I needed to make me happy. Anyway, I've got a little bit of money in my pocket now, and Davion's going to get to medical school, so maybe it's time to settle myself into something different altogether. Just Tadeo and me, being…normal."

It felt like the bottom was falling out of her world. Everything was totally whirling out of control, getting further and further away in the distance. She was losing Coulson. Losing Tadeo. Not that she ever had them, but still… She couldn't even imagine what life here would be like without them. "What about your patients?" she asked, trying to sound steady when nothing inside her was.

"I have an idea that your hospital will have enough doctors coming and going so that the medical care here will be well covered. We've gone from famine to feast, medically, which is all I ever wanted in the first place."

"But you're part of that feast, Coulson. The people here want you, not the visiting doctors who'll be coming to the hospital. You're the medicine in the area and they don't want an outsider."

"They're good people. They'll be glad to have anyone who wants to practice here."

"But my visiting doctors are coming for the children." Weak argument, she knew. "Not to staff a general medical clinic."

"You'd recruit doctors who would turn away a patient, even if that patient isn't the specific one they've come to see?" He shook his head. "I don't think so, Red. You're going to bring in people who are just like you and your father. So I don't need to be here any longer."

She wasn't sure what was causing all this, but the one thing she did know was that Coulson hadn't had these feelings before she'd come here. Which made her feel terrible. It was like she'd ripped the dream right out from under him, and that had never been her intention. In fact, she had been looking forward to a shared medical community because...because she'd let herself dream a little, too. Dream of something beyond the hospital and the clinic and the work. Or maybe it was a dream that encompassed all that, and more. But she'd never been demonstrative. She remembered sitting there that day her parents had walked away, just watching them. No crying out, no begging them to stay or come back. She'd sat in her child-size wheelchair with silent tears and watched them leave. And in her little-girl heart, she'd known they weren't coming back. Yet, all these years, she'd wondered what would have happened if she'd asked them to stay. That wasn't taking anything away from her real father, the man who wanted her. The big question always lingered, though. *What if?* "You can't go," she said, knowing she couldn't live with another *what if.*

"But what if I can't stay?"

"Because of me? Is that what this is about? I'm here, my father's here, now you're feeling...edged out?"

He spun round, marched out of the water and straight at her. "No one edges me out, Red. But nothing's working like I'd planned and I'm thinking that it would be easier to try it again somewhere else."

"Nothing ever works out like anybody plans, Coulson. We want things. We create fantasies around what we want and those turn into our goals. But how many little girls really do grow up to be fairy princesses, and how many little boys really do become cowboys or firemen? Life happens, things change. People change, and their goals change. That's just the way it is. The thing is, you can let your heart keep breaking the way I know yours is right now, or you can start over right where you are. God knows, I've had to do that a few times in my life. And you know what? Each time my direction changes, I see something better out there for me. Coming to this island wasn't my dream. I wanted this hospital, but I always pictured it in Chicago or London or Montreal. And it was huge, with resources you can't even imagine. But my father started going blind and everything was different. Everything changed. I knew he couldn't function in the hospital of my dreams, knew he wouldn't be able to cope in a large city setting. So because his heart was here, I knew this was where I had to be, too.

"And the hospital I'd planned…nothing like the one I'm getting. But the one I'm getting, now that I'm almost there, is so much better. My vision for it changed and I'm glad it did because…" She swallowed hard. This was the part that scared her, but no more *what ifs*. Never again. "Because I met you, and you're the best thing that's ever happened to me. I fell in love with you here, and I want to stay in love with you here. You, me…Tadeo. But if you can't be here, if you absolutely can't be here then I'll go, too." She hadn't expected that part, but it was true. She would go. "If you'll have me."

His eyes widened, but apart from that there was no big show of emotion. Not like she'd hoped for, not like she'd wanted. Because this was the place where they should have fallen into each other's arms. But he was still towering over her, stiffly. Was it because she'd misread him so badly? Maybe he didn't want a cancer survivor because cancer always did hover. Or maybe she'd seen something where nothing existed. "And if you won't have me…" she said, after a big gulp, not sure what words came next. Not sure how to extricate herself gracefully from the moment. "Then I'll just have to…"

"What, Red?" he asked, as a spark of amusement leapt to his eyes. "What will you just *have* to do?"

"Actually, I never planned to get this far into the conversation." She rose up to her knees. "And I'm debating my options. One would be…" She beckoned him down with a crooked finger. "There's room for two on my towel."

"Barely," he said, stepping in even closer.

"Barely makes it better, doesn't it? Or is this…" What if…what if he didn't want her? "…just foolish? I mean, we've never…not even so much as a kiss, and here I am presuming more than you've ever hinted at. But life is short, Coulson. You may only get one chance to go after what you want, so I have to know. Could we do this? You and me together? Give it a try and see what happens?"

He shook his head. "Can't do that, Red."

Her heart sank. She'd had her big, brave moment and now it was time to retreat. Cut her losses. Hide her heart. "I understand," she said, wishing she could bury herself in the sand.

"Understand what?" he asked, kneeling down in the sand next to her.

Instinctively, she pulled away from him "We didn't even have a relationship. Not like most people would define it. But I thought…you know, it doesn't matter what I thought because I was wrong."

He nodded. "Or maybe you weren't."

"So you're staying?" she asked.

"I don't know." He sighed heavily. "Don't know anything."

Now, this was awkward. She didn't know how she could

be on the same island with him, let alone in the same little village, seeing him day after day, knowing what a fool she'd made of herself.

"If I stay, can you manage with me on one side of your fence, you on the other? Would that work for you, Red?"

So he was considering staying, but not with her. In answer to his question, she scooted herself back away from him, then stood, grabbed her towel and poised herself to march off with whatever dignity she could still muster. But he grabbed her by the arm. Stopped her. Spun her around to face him. And damn it, even his touch, as impersonal as he intended it, gave her chills. She couldn't control herself.

"Answer me, Red. Would that work for you?"

"You know what, Coulson? I gave it a shot…my best shot. But I misfired and there's no second shot lined up for me. OK? You do what you want. Stay, leave. I don't care because I learned a long time ago that when you care too much, you get hurt. And that's something I can live without."

"The caring or the hurting?"

His eyes were suddenly so gentle she had to look away or be lost for ever.

"Red? *Erin*?"

"Don't do this to me," she begged.

"I'm not doing anything."

"You are, though. Don't you see? You're hurting me. Taking Tadeo, and leaving here. I don't know how I can get through that. And don't tell me that I'm strong or that some other visiting doctor will take your place because that's not going to happen."

"But you are strong. You just don't know it."

"And that's supposed to be good enough? Erin Glover is strong, she can take care of herself? Well, it's *not* good enough. I live in a safe world. I have since the first time my father gave me a piece of candy and asked me my name. And this…all this isn't safe." She pointed to the beach, to the trees, to the blue hospital building in the distance, to the crazy patchwork-colored fence. "It scares me. You scare me. And more than anything, my feelings for you scare me because…"

"Tell me, Red. Say it out loud."

She swallowed hard. "Because I didn't know those kinds of feelings could exist. You're not safe, Coulson. If anything, you're the unsafest man I've ever known, and I should have fallen in love with someone who was safe, but I fell in love with you instead."

He chuckled. "I'm not sure whether to be insulted or flattered. The lady claims she loves me by telling me she should have fallen in love with someone else. I've had a few women profess various feelings for me in one way or another, but never quite so grudgingly."

"So I lack social skills."

He pulled her into his arms. Held her tight. Just lingered in the feel of her body pressed to his for a moment…a sensation he wanted to last for ever. "It's not about giving it a try. It's about doing it. Also, simply doing…*us*. Your social skills are just fine," he said, on a sigh. "All the social skills I need in my woman."

"Your woman?" she asked.

His woman. Absolutely, definitely his woman. "Trouble at first sight. I knew when I set eyes on that red hair you were going to be trouble for me, and I don't mean anything to do with the hospital."

"But you haven't… Never. Not anything."

"You mean, not this…?" Leaning forward, he ran his fingers lightly down her neck, stopping just at her collarbone, where he bent and placed a row of delicate kisses, a trail of them that didn't stop until he reached her shoulder.

"Not that," she said on a shiver.

"And I'm assuming none of this either?" His next kisses went to the swell just above her breast. Harder kisses, ones that lingered a little longer. Ones he didn't want to stop but knew he had to because even this innocent little moment with Erin was almost more than he could bear.

"None of those either," she murmured. "And that's a pity," she said, nuzzling herself a little harder against him, "because those kinds of kisses are usually rewarded with something like this."

In an instant her fingers were woven around his neck, and she was standing on tiptoe in the sand to reach his lips with kisses that were neither tentative nor conditional. Meeting her tongue with his, feeling the wet, satiny heat merging with the pure, honey taste of her, Adam pressed his fingers into the small of her back, pulling her closer, harder. Then they settled into a fiery kiss—one with a beginning and a promise, one that promised even more passion and committed to everything. One that settled Erin back down on the towel and showed Adam once and for all that there was definitely room enough for two.

"Coulson," she said a while later, when their passion had gone as far as it could on a public, even though semi-secluded beach. "I wanted…I mean, I never thought we would…"

He shushed her with a finger to her lips, and she responded by pulling his finger into her mouth and sucking.

"You're going to get us both in a lot of trouble if you keep that up," he warned, even though he did nothing to stop it.

"Could be fun," she said, almost shyly.

That was something he liked about her…*loved* about her, that shy sweet sexiness that was as spicy as anything he'd ever known. "Let me guess. You're such a good girl, you've never gotten into trouble before, have you?"

"Define trouble," she said, her shyness turning to daring as she looked up at him. "Show me, Coulson. Show me trouble."

His answer was a moan as he scooped her up into his arms. "It's on the other side of the cove, in my private beach cabana."

"I like private," she said, on a sigh.

It was hours, days, maybe an eternity before she realized that she might be missed. "I think I should go," she said, pulling the gauzy sheet up around her, not so much to shield herself as he knew every inch of her intimately now but more to separate herself from the moment to make their parting easier. This was a wonderful place, his cabana. A small little beach shack he'd built that she never wanted to leave. But reality rained down. It was time.

"I think you should stay awhile longer."

His bare backside was facing toward her and even as a physician, who'd seen the beautiful lines of a man before, she couldn't take her eyes off him. Sleek, perfect. Her lover for a moment, but beyond that… "If I stay, you'll break my heart." With his beauty, with the emptiness of words not yet spoken, words she desperately wanted to hear. But there'd been no mention of him staying on the island, or changing his mind, not even that he loved her, and she could feel the dull ache of it beginning to settle in again. Being his woman was wonderful, but not enough. "And in the end, Coulson, I have to figure out a way to be able to function here." He didn't turn round, didn't move. Simply stood there, every masculine inch of him, against the backdrop of a white sandy beach and, beyond that, an eternity of blue. Blue was a color of hope, though. That was why she'd chosen it for her hospital. Yet now, when she saw all the blue just outside the cabana, she felt a swell of discouragement. Even sadness for another loss, for someone else walking out of her life.

"You've never called me Adam," he said. "Why's that?"

She sat up, pulled her knees up and rested her chin on them, thinking about it for a moment. The truth was, she didn't know. Didn't have any idea. "Habit, maybe," she finally said, not totally convinced.

Eventually, after what felt like an eternity, he turned to her, yet he kept himself half-hidden in the shadows of the filmy curtains. "Maybe the same reason I've called you Red since the day we met…to keep the relationship impersonal."

"But we've changed since that day. Both of us have."

"Have we? Have we really?" He heaved a sigh then returned to the bed and crawled in next to her, yet avoided any touch, any closeness. "The thing is, I know why I've called you Red. I wanted to be impersonal. That was my goal. I wanted to stay detached, even disinterested because…well, I guess you can say that once bitten, twice shy, but that's a cliché and it's not really the truth. For a lot of reasons, it was easy to hide behind the failure of my first marriage, and always hold it out there in front of me as a shield. I didn't want to get involved, and that's the honest truth. I was good without involvement, and my life was easier when it didn't have to take someone else into consideration…someone who would let me down, someone I would let down. In my little closed-minded patch of the world, that was good. Then there you were and I knew the instant I saw you that you were going to disrupt everything in my life. Totally turn it all upside down, probably in ways I couldn't imagine. Like I said, I knew it that first day at the bar, and I've known it and seen it every day since. And the thing is, part of me wanted that upheaval… was probably even ready for it. But most of me really just wanted to keep that shield up. Except you have a habit of slipping right through. Every single time I thought I had my defenses up, you simply walked straight in. And you do it so naturally…Erin. You walk gracefully through life and that's a rare gift. It's also frightening to a man who *wants* to be set in his ways."

"Let me guess. Nobody wants that more than you do, right?"

He chuckled. "Right. And, I'll admit it. I didn't want to get involved…to get to the place where we are right now, because I knew if we did, and for whatever reason, we couldn't sustain it, someone would lose, something would change. Your life, my life…hopes and dreams. Funny thing was, last night, when I actually started thinking in terms of really changing my life or leaving here, that's when it finally dawned on me that it's not about losing or even changing. I lost so much to my first wife and I didn't want to lose this, too. So when you were Red, you were…"

"Impersonal? Nothing you could lose?"

"Definitely impersonal. And maybe that was a little bit of my battle still playing out. But you know what? I can walk away from here, start a new life, and that's what it will be…a new life. Not the outcome of a battle—win, lose or draw. Old conditioning dying hard, I suppose. Or, like you said, old habits."

"But can't you start that new life here?"

"Can I?"

"There's nothing stopping you from doing whatever you want, so I don't understand."

"Yes, I think you do, *Erin*. Maybe you're not ready to

say it out loud, but you do understand. So answer this. You still call me Coulson because..."

"Because I didn't know you wanted me to call you something else."

He shook his head. "That's not it."

"Then, like I said, it's a habit."

She pulled the gauzy sheet up to her throat and started to slide away from him, but he reached out and held her there. Still separated, but so close the awareness of her bare flesh on his fought to distract him in ways he was only just learning that Erin could distract him as no one ever had. "Say the words, Erin. You have to say the words. We *both* need to hear them."

"There aren't any words, because I don't know what you're talking about. And this is a stupid conversation, going on and on about what I call you. I need to go and see the architect, then talk to my dad about—"

"Tell me, Erin." This time his voice was purposely firm. "Just tell me."

She looked up at the ceiling, hoping the tears that so wanted to spring to her eyes would roll back in. Then she took a deep breath. "I call you Coulson because it won't hurt so much when you leave me. Because if I call you anything other than Coulson, I'm vulnerable to something I can't control, and I'm never going to be vulnerable that way again. I won't let it happen."

"Why, Erin?" he asked, his voice gentle.

"Because trusting someone, and being vulnerable to them, hurt me worse than the cancer ever could have. Because in the moments when I didn't know if I was going to live or die, the pain of my broken heart was worse than anything the doctors were putting me through. I've had all the love in the world from the most wonderful person, more than most people ever get, but it doesn't quite heal me. So if I don't…" She batted at the tears finally breaking loose. "If I don't make myself vulnerable, then…"

"Then nobody breaks Erin's heart again."

She nodded.

"But you trust your father, and you certainly have a relationship with him where you're nothing but vulnerable."

"Because he chose me. He knew…everything. Knew that I might die. Knew that I could cost him so much money with my care. Yet he chose me anyway. No one else ever did. Not my birth parents, not any of my friends…they all ran away from me. But my father always ran toward me because he chose me."

"Does he know that you never quite healed?"

She shook her head. "I'd never hurt him."

"Or maybe you're afraid he'd run away, too, if he knew? That he'd be disappointed in you somehow for still having that little bit of fear inside you that he might just walk away and, because of that, he would?"

Her bottom lip trembled. Tears poured down her face, but she didn't speak. Couldn't. There were no more words, not in her head, not in her heart. Not when someone knew her soul the way Coulson did. Which made her utterly vulnerable to him in every way. There was nothing more to hide, no other feelings to have.

"What they did to you was a horrible thing, Erin. I don't even know what to say about that. But let me ask you one thing. You love Tadeo, that goes without saying. And he's a sick little boy, with a very difficult future ahead of him. If I weren't here to take him and all he had was you, would you leave him? For whatever reason, take your pick, would you walk away from him?"

Her eyes flew open, registering total shock. "Of course I wouldn't. If I were lucky enough to have that little boy as my son I'd move heaven and earth to keep him."

"Like your father did for you. Like father, like daughter, Erin. It's not in the blood, it's in the love. In the heart. And *he* did move heaven and earth."

"Sometimes I wonder why," she said, sniffling.

Finally, he pulled her into his arms and tilted her face up. "The same question I've been asking myself for the past few days, but the answer was always there. I was just trying not to see it."

"What question?"

"What if I choose you, too, Erin?"

"But you didn't. You chose to take Tadeo and leave."

"In my own moment of vulnerability, I think. Trying to avoid getting hurt. But that's the thing about a bad choice. Once you know it's bad, it's easy to change."

"You're staying?"

"I'm choosing. You. Tadeo. Your father and even Mrs Meecham. Miss Francelle Henry. Davion and Trinique. Breeon, Leron and Algernon Adam Edward. This life. That awful blue building…"

"Blue is good," she said. "It's a color of hope."

"Would you choose me, Erin, if I don't change my mind about the color?"

"I would choose you, Adam. No matter what kind of boring colors you like, I would choose you."

"Red is nice," he said, running his fingers through her hair. "It's my new favorite color. Although I'll admit I'm suddenly not as fond of plain old white as I used to be." He pulled the gauzy *white* sheet off her and dropped it on the floor beside the bed, at the same time arching wicked eyebrows at her. "Nope, don't like it at all."

Ten months later

"See what I can do?" Tadeo yelled at his admiring public… his soon-to-be mother, father, grandfather and his adopted aunt, Mrs Meecham, not to mention Miss Francelle Henry, who'd moved into one of the guest cottages one day several months ago and had never moved out. She'd already become a vital part of the community, working at the hospital every day, playing with the children, taking care of Tadeo.

"What can you do?" Erin called back to him, as the rest of this wonderful family sat at the picnic table, enjoying the cool of the afternoon as a few friends prepared the beach for the festivities. It was hard to believe it was here, but they'd decided to wait until Tadeo was well on his way to full recovery. So this day marked three special events: Tadeo's official release as a patient from the Algernon Glover Hospital; her wedding; and the signing of Tadeo's adoption papers. In another hour she'd be Adam's wife and shortly after that Tadeo's mother. And in such a casual way…the way it should be. A stroll to the beach with her family, joined by a few close friends, then exchanging vows at sunset…

"This!" In the blink of an eye Tadeo popped a wheelie in his wheelchair.

Erin gasped, of course, while Adam laughed. Algernon, who still had sight but not so much these days, was the one who jumped up and shouted, "That's my grandson! I taught him how to do that." He headed straight for Tadeo to give him the old high-five.

"They're incorrigible," Erin said, wondering if there was a better word to describe contentment. So far, in all these months, she hadn't been able to think of one.

"It's only going to get worse," Adam whispered in her ear. "When your father finds out about the next one on the way, there's going to be no stopping him."

"I've got a while before it shows, so let's just keep our secret a little longer." She gazed out at her dad, who was

heading off toward the beach with Tadeo...for the big surprise *before* the wedding. She had an idea her dad already
knew that he was going to be a grandfather again, maybe
that's why the blindness hadn't yet overtaken him. Who
knew? Or maybe his happiness and newfound purpose,
including Tadeo, had something to do with it. Whatever
the case, she suspected he was giving Adam and her time
to enjoy the wonderful feeling between themselves of becoming parents for the second time.

As for Tadeo, he wasn't being quite so patient. She'd
wanted to keep the surprise a surprise a while longer, maybe
give Adam his wedding gift in a more private moment, but
Tadeo had insisted it had to be now. He wanted a big public
presentation, and there was no way she could refuse him,
as he'd been making plans for days.

"Look, I think I'll go and walk through the hospital
before I come down to the beach, see if anybody needs
anything before we head off on our honeymoon."

"Honeymoon? What honeymoon?"

"Well, I've been thinking about that. I know this nice
little cabana on the other side of your beach. Might have
stocked it with a bottle of champagne...the non-alcoholic
kind."

"Ooh, tempt me more, Dr Coulson."

"And I have this awesome stethoscope. Thought maybe
we could practice listening to each other's hearts."

"And...?"

"Yam bammys. Had Kevan make them fresh just a little
while ago."

"You had me with the yam bammys, Doctor. But let's
skip the first part, where you go to the hospital. Tadeo's
waiting on the beach, not very being patient about it, and
the hospital is doing just fine without us." Better than fine.
The Algernon Hospital, as people were calling it, was fully

functional, and she had so many visiting volunteer doctors she almost felt lazy at times. It was good and she already had plans to expand, thanks to a generous donation from Miss Henry. More than that, her father had actually chosen Adam's clinic over the hospital as far as where he wanted to practice medicine, maybe because the small setting made him feel more confident. Whatever the case, with her dad's help, Adam was in mid-plan to build a small general hospital himself. All good, again.

But best of all was Tadeo. As soon as she and Adam were married, they would sign the adoption papers for Tadeo. His heart operations were behind him now, his burns had healed beautifully, and all he had to do was rest and recover and adjust to being part of a real family. The resting part was going to be tough, though, because her dad loved having a grandson. They were best friends, inseparable, and as she'd just witnessed with the wheelchair, her dad had a few tricks up his sleeve for Tadeo.

Better than good. Perfect. A life fulfilled, finally. She rubbed her still-flat belly. Better than perfect. More than fulfilled.

"Well, if Tadeo's involved in the surprise, that rules out several things that come to mind," Adam said.

"Hold that thought, Doctor. For after the bammys."

"Well, they look like a wild bunch." He pointed to the parade of family and friends all headed for the beach. "I have a feeling the bammys are going to be very cold by the time this crowd gets through partying."

"Then we party with them. And I did promise Miss Henry that you'd save the second dance for her."

"And our honeymoon…"

"Will wait a few hours." She stood on tiptoe and brushed a quick kiss to his lips. "And it's not like we haven't had a few honeymoons already." She took his hand and held it to her belly. "Very successful ones."

Adam chuckled. "I feel a girl in there. Red hair, feisty, stubborn."

"Is that a guess, or some kind of divining talent?"

"A dream. They do come true, Red."

"Yes, they do, don't they, Coulson?" OK, so he did still call her Red sometimes, and sometimes she still called him Coulson. But they knew it was only habit, and part of her didn't want to let go of the habit because that would be like letting go of part of their past. Still, they never ever called each other Red or Coulson behind closed doors. "So, what if she doesn't have red hair?"

"What color could it be?" he asked, as they strolled toward the beach, toward the beginning of so many wonderful things.

"Could be blue." In the end, the hospital had stayed blue, and while her husband had yet to admit a fondness for it, he wasn't quite so vocal against it either.

"Not blue!" he teased. "Anything but blue."

"Well, you'd better change that attitude, because I've got some blue for you." As they stepped out from a clump of trees, everyone was standing in a line. Serek and Alvinnia. Tyjon, Ennis and Willeen Clarke. Davion and Trinique. The whole Edward family. Miss Francelle Henry. Mrs Meecham. Her father. Tadeo…her life, her family. They were pointing to the most hideously colored boat. Not one, not two, not even three shades of blue, but five, all in some stage of peeling.

"It's a…" Adam choked.

"A wooden 1951 Lyman Islander. I know it's not the one your grandfather gave you, but it's new memories, Adam. You and Tadeo, and our second child…the one with the blue hair. You'll have brand-new memories, and they'll be good. I promise you, they'll be good, too."

"I don't know what to say," he choked out, standing there, holding on to his wife, looking at everything he had in his life. "I *don't* know what to say."

"That you love blue? Because according to my renovation estimation, *Stella II* is probably going to be blue until your second *grandchild* at least."

"Not *Stella II*," he said, pulling her into his arms. "*Stella Blue*, and I love blue. But not as much as I love Red."

They kissed, of course, in front of a yelling, applauding audience. "So, Tadeo," Algernon said, as Erin and Adam finally pulled away from each other and headed toward the boat, where they would exchange their marriage vows. "Any bets? Are you going to get a baby brother or sister?"

Tadeo looked at his parents, and smiled over the worst-kept secret ever. "Probably both."

0411/03a

Medical Romance™

HER LITTLE SECRET
by Carol Marinelli

At Eastern Beach Hospital new doctor Nick Roberts' fun-loving
attitude is so infectious that nurse Alison Carter is unwillingly hooked.
One night with Nick leaves Alison with a new zest for life—and one
rather more unexpected gift…

THE DOCTOR'S DAMSEL IN DISTRESS
by Janice Lynn

There's something about nurse Madison's unawakened sex appeal
that has Dr Levi Fielding *desperate* to have her in his arms. So when
Levi saves Madison's life at a hospital picnic, he knows it's a white
knight moment he'll take *full* advantage of…

THE TAMING OF DR ALEX DRAYCOTT
by Joanna Neil

Dr Alex Draycott has plenty on her plate—even before she meets
the rebelliously charming Dr Callum Brooksby! Feisty Alex can
handle a challenge—but it seems Callum is out to tame her heart…

THE MAN BEHIND THE BADGE
by Sharon Archer

However new-doc-in-town Kayla Morgan tries, she can't resist being
impressed by law-enforcing Tom Jamieson! But taking a bullet in the
line of duty has made cop Tom rethink his work hard/party harder
lifestyle—will he ever let Kayla see the real man behind the badge?

On sale from 6th May 2011
Don't miss out!

Available at WHSmith, Tesco, ASDA, Eason and all good bookshops
www.millsandboon.co.uk

2 FREE BOOKS
AND A SURPRISE GIFT

We would like to take this opportunity to thank you for reading this Mills & Boon® book by offering you the chance to take TWO more specially selected books from the Medical™ series absolutely FREE! We're also making this offer to introduce you to the benefits of the Mills & Boon® Book Club™—

- **FREE home delivery**
- **FREE gifts and competitions**
- **FREE monthly Newsletter**
- **Exclusive Mills & Boon Book Club offers**
- **Books available before they're in the shops**

Accepting these FREE books and gift places you under no obligation to buy, you may cancel at any time, even after receiving your free books. Simply complete your details below and return the entire page to the address below. You don't even need a stamp!

YES Please send me 2 free Medical books and a surprise gift. I understand that unless you hear from me, I will receive 5 superb new stories every month including two 2-in-1 books priced at £5.30 each and a single book priced at £3.30, postage and packing free. I am under no obligation to purchase any books and may cancel my subscription at any time. The free books and gift will be mine to keep in any case.

Ms/Mrs/Miss/Mr _____ Initials _____

_____

Surname _____

Address _____

_____

_____ Postcode _____

E-mail _____

Send this whole page to: Mills & Boon Book Club, Free Book Offer, FREEPOST NAT 10298, Richmond, TW9 1BR

Offer valid in UK only and is not available to current Mills & Boon Book Club subscribers to this series. Overseas and Eire please write for details. We reserve the right to refuse an application and applicants must be aged 18 years or over. Only one application per household. Terms and prices subject to change without notice. Offer expires 30th June 2011. As a result of this application, you may receive offers from Harlequin (UK) and other carefully selected companies. If you would prefer not to share in this opportunity please write to The Data Manager, PO Box 676, Richmond, TW9 1WU.

Mills & Boon® is a registered trademark owned by Harlequin (UK) Limited.
Medical™ is being used as a trademark. The Mills & Boon® Book Club™ is being used as a trademark.